ALEX CAGE
CLEAN FAST-PACED ACTION THRILLERS

JOIN THE READER'S LIST

Get the latest releases and exclusive giveaways - sign up to
the Alex Cage Reader List:

www.AlexCage.com/signup

ALSO BY ALEX CAGE

Leroy Silver Series

Contracts & Bullets

Aloha & Bullets

Politics Thieves & Bullets

Orlando Black Series

Carolina Dance

Bayside Boom

Bet on Black

Get the latest releases and exclusive giveaways, sign up to the Alex Cage Reader List.

www.AlexCage.com/signup

ALOHA & BULLETS

A LEROY SILVER ADVENTURE

ALEX CAGE

WHEN SOMEONE HAS a head start, chasing them on foot can be challenging, especially while wearing a tailored suit and a pair of Stacy Adams. This is what Leroy Silver was pondering as he pursued a lanky, red-haired, freckled face man through the streets of Lower Manhattan. It was just after noon when Silver spotted him in the lobby of the office building where he worked. The freckle-faced young man had been snapping pictures, and since the company didn't allow picture taking, for national security reasons, Silver made his way across the lobby and toward the man to inform him of the company's policy. But when the lanky guy saw him approaching, he jetted out of the building and up the street.

Silver dodged and threaded around pedestrians. "Hey, I just want to talk!" he called to the young man.

The kid just glanced over his shoulder and kept running. He shoved through a crowd and continued across an intersection, but the red crosswalk light indicated he shouldn't have. A white car honked as it sped by, almost hitting him. And before the redhead guy made it to the opposite side, an SUV screeched to a halt, nudging him off balance and sending him flopping to the pavement.

The man crawled to his knees and inspected the now detached lens of the camera that hung around his neck. "Ah man!"

Silver caught a whiff of burnt rubber as he grabbed him by his jacket collar, yanked him off the street, and threw him against the wall. "Who are you?"

"Let go of me!" the young guy said as he pushed against Silver's arms.

Silver put his forearm to the kid's chest, then used his free hand to pat him down. He felt the young man's chest expand and contract and the heat from his exhales breeze across his forearm.

A curvy woman with straight brown hair exited the SUV and walked to them with both hands covering her mouth. "Oh my goodness, are you crazy!" she said to the kid.

Keeping the guy pressed against the wall, Silver turned to face her. "Ma'am please get back in your vehicle," he said, extending his arm between her and redheaded guy.

"This lunatic ran out in the middle of the street."

"I know, I'll take care of it."

"I'm sorry. He was chasing me," the young man said, nodding at Silver.

"Shut up," Silver told him.

"You're not hurt, are you? Because this was your fault," the woman said.

"No, he's not hurt," Silver answered.

"How do you know that?" the lanky man asked.

"I said shut up."

Multiple cars honked. Silver glanced at the street and saw a line of vehicles behind the woman's SUV. "Ms., you have to move your car," he said.

"Okay. You don't look hurt, so I'm leaving. But next time, pay attention to the light," the curvy woman said before walking back to her car.

Silver continued to pat the young man down and found an ID card in his front pocket. *The Big A Tribune* sat in bold print at the top of the card, and at the center was an image of the kid with the name *Bobby Hartley* and the title *Associate Reporter*.

Silver released his captive. "So Bobby, you work for that small newspaper no one ever reads. Question is, why did you run?" he said before tossing the ID card to Bobby.

"I ran because you were chasing me."

"I was only going to tell you that taking pictures in the building's not allowed."

"Well, it doesn't matter now," Bobby said while lifting his busted camera.

"Like the lady said, that's your fault. Now, get out of here."

Bobby scoffed. "Jerk," he said, shaking his head and continuing up the sidewalk.

Silver watched Bobby until the young man disappeared into a crowd of passersby before making the walk back to the office. When he arrived at the front entrance, the doors slid apart and a pale, full-figured man in a security guard uniform stepped out.

"Boss, did you catch him?" the man asked.

"Yeah, I got him, Greg," Silver answered.

Greg glanced behind Silver. "Well, where is he?"

Silver shook his head. "Don't worry about it. He was just a reporter," he said as he walked past Greg and to the doors.

"Wow, you chased him for nothing. You shouldn't be working so hard just before your vacation, boss."

"Tell me about it. Next time, I'm letting you do the chasing."

Silver heard a slapping noise behind him as he entered the lobby, and when he glanced over his shoulder, he saw Greg drumming his belly with his hands.

"I don't know. I've got to get this body chase ready first."

Silver laughed. "We can work on that. I'm taking a break. I'll be in my office."

"Sure thing, boss."

Silver continued across the concrete, polished lobby floor and to the elevator. He pressed the up arrow, and a floral scent struck his nose as the elevator doors opened. The fifth floor was his stop. The west wing of the floor housed I.T. support and surveillance staff, while most of the security team sat in the east wing. Silver headed to the far east wall, passing a few offices and conference rooms on his way. In the corner was a spacious office with large glass windows. Printed on the office door's plaque were the words, *Cush Industries*, and printed below that, *Leroy Silver, Head of Security*. Inside the office, a teal-colored carpet with circular designs covered the floor. The furniture consisted of a desk with an executive chair behind it and two guest chairs in front of it. On the opposite side of the room, a sofa rested against the wall perpendicular to a window with a view that framed most of Manhattan.

Silver plopped into the executive chair and sighed. "That was the most excitement I've had in months," he uttered to himself as his gaze went to a picture on his desk. The picture showed Silver side-hugging a woman with long, curly hair. Her skin had color but was noticeably lighter next to Silver's brown skin. The two had big smiles on their faces and were standing in Central Park. "I wonder how your day is going, Jules."

At that thought, Silver's desk phone rang.

"Cush Industries, Leroy Silver speaking," he answered.

A man chuckled. "I had to hear it for myself," the familiar voice said.

"Matt Anderson, how have you been?"

"Good, but when I heard the great Leroy Silver resorted to the cubicle lifestyle, I couldn't resist calling." Anderson continued laughing.

"Ha-ha. It's honest work, and it keeps me doing something."

"Yeah, but we both know a man with your skillset doesn't belong in an office. I bet you're bored."

Silver exhaled. "To tears. The funny thing is, the boredom is actually draining me."

"You can always come back to the unit."

"No, I'm done working for the government. And like I told you, some orders I just can't follow."

"I know. Just remember you always have a friend here."

"I will."

"Hey, maybe we can get together sometime this weekend and catch up."

"I can't. Jules and I are heading to Hawaii."

"That's right. How long will you be there?"

"We're leaving out early tomorrow, and we'll be back in a week."

"You two have been spending a lot of time together."

"We're just friends."

"Yeah, okay. Well, I think you'll really enjoy that resort, but look, have fun on your trip, and I'll talk to you when you get back."

"Okay man, talk to you later," Silver said, before placing the phone back on the hook.

As he leaned backward in the chair, he heard another

phone ring. This time, it was his personal cell phone. The name *Kirby Cush* displayed on the screen.

"Hello Ms. Cush," he answered.

"Good afternoon, Mr. Silver. How's everything? Still quiet?" Kirby said.

"Well, earlier we had a wannabe reporter in the lobby taking pictures, but other than that, things have been quiet."

"That's great. Quiet is good."

"Kirby, I'm happy you called. I need to talk to you about something."

"Wonderful, because I need to have a word with you too."

"Sure. What is it?"

"It's—it's better if we talk in person. I know you're leaving for your trip tomorrow, so can you cut out early and stop by the mansion on your way home?"

"Yes, ma'am."

"Ma'am?" Kirby laughed. "We had this talk before Leroy," she said, stretching out the syllables of his name. "You don't have to call me ma'am; you're older than I am."

"Just trying to show a little respect."

"I know. That's one of the things I admire about you. But anyway, I'll see you in a little while—oh wait. You had something you wanted to tell me?"

"We'll talk about it when we meet."

"You sure?"

"Yes ma—Yes. Just yes."

Kirby giggled. "Okay, I'll see you then," she said before ending the call.

An hour and a half later, Silver called for a driver to bring one of the company's town cars to the front of the building. He slid into the back seat and instructed the driver to take him to Kirby's home. They arrived at a massive estate surrounded by an enormous gate that made it nearly impossible to see what was on the other side. The driver rang the bell at the gate and looked at the intercom speaker in anticipation, as if he had done it before. Eight seconds passed and nothing happened. The driver rang the bell again, but still no answer.

"They must not hear the bell," he said to Silver.

Silver looked at the driver, then the gate's bell panel. "Hm," he huffed as he exited the car. He circled around the trunk and walked to the panel.

A digital keypad protruded next to the bell button. Silver pressed the number for the code, and a couple seconds later, the gate buzzed open. Silver entered the car, and they drove through and onto a brick driveway. A large mansion sitting on a huge plot of land welcomed them, and at the front entrance, a gold sedan sat parked with the trunk door open. The driver stopped a few yards behind the car and Silver saw the mansion's front door wide open.

"Wait here," he told the driver before exiting the car, removing his Glock 22, and aiming it at the front door of the house. He made it five feet from the door before a petite Asian woman stepped out.

The woman jumped. "Leroy! What are you doing? Trying to scare me to death?"

Silver released a sharp exhale. "Oh, Semy."

"Yes, it's me, Semy," she said, brushing past him and walking to the back of the sedan.

"Sorry," Silver said, as he holstered his gun. "Where's everyone, and why is the door open?"

Semy removed a suitcase and a laptop case from the back before shutting the trunk door. "Everyone is inside, and the door is open because I just got here," she answered as she walked past Silver again.

"Need a hand?" he asked as she passed.

"Nope, got it."

Silver waved at the driver and followed Semy into the house. She sat her bags on the foyer floor.

"Moving in?" Silver said, stepping inside and closing the door behind himself.

Semy brushed her short, straight, black hair behind her ear and sighed as she placed her hands on her hips. "Yep, only for a few days, though. Kirby and I are going to enjoy some girl-time," she said with a smile.

"Oh, you mean like a slumber party? You're telling me the PD gave you time off for that?"

Semy tilted her head and poked her lips. "Do we look like we're twelve, and I'm entitled to my personal leave."

Silver hunched his shoulders.

"Whatever, Leroy," Semy said as she removed her hands from her hips. "For your information, we girls will spend the next few days at the spa, shopping and pampering ourselves."

Footsteps knocked from the opposite side of the foyer. "I'm sorry ma'am, let me get your luggage," the butler said as he approached Silver and Semy.

"Not a problem, I got it," Semy said.

The man picked up her bags. "But I insist; you're a guest." He then turned to Silver and nodded, "Good afternoon, Mr. Silver. Ms. Cush has been expecting you. She's in the kitchen."

Silver returned the nod. "Thanks, Stan."

The butler then faced Semy. "I'll take these to your usual

room," he said before walking past the staircase and toward a hall.

"Usual room?" Silver said. "You might as well move in."

"Shut up," Semy said. "Kirby's my girl. Like a sister to me."

"Well, let me go see what your sista wants."

The two walked across the foyer and to the kitchen. A tall blonde stood at the kitchen island, and standing with her, were a young maid and two security guards. The group wore smiles and laughed.

"No wonder I had to buzz myself through. Half of the staff is in here. Kirby, you approved this?"

The tall blonde looked at Silver with pursed lips. Her eyes were blue with a hint of green. "There you are," she said, walking to where he and Semy stood. "We can talk in my study," she said to Silver. She then turned to Semy and pointed. "You ready, girl?"

Semy pointed back at her. "Oh, I'm ready."

"Let me go handle this business, and we'll get this party started."

The two giggled.

"Oh brother," Silver said, before walking out of the kitchen.

Kirby followed him, and the two walked upstairs and through a set of double doors. They entered a spacious room with tall bookshelves and picture-covered walls. Kirby walked behind a desk at the far end of the room, opened a drawer, and removed an envelope. She handed it to Silver.

"What's this?" he asked.

"Leroy, when you first came to me, it was by high recommendation. And in these past few months, I've witnessed firsthand why that was the case. You are good—no, great at what you do. I trust you and feel my company and I are much safer when you're around. You're an incredible head of security and an even more incredible friend. So, I just wanted to give you something to show my gratitude as your boss and friend."

Silver opened the envelope and saw a check and number with many zeros behind it. "Are you sure? This is a lot of money. You know I'm not hurting; I received a pension from my previous job."

Kirby shook her head as she stepped closer to him. "I'm positive. And I'm not concerned about how your previous employer compensated you. You've earned this for the hard work you've done for Cush Industries."

"Okay, well, I'm not going to argue with the boss," Silver said.

Kirby hugged him. "Thank you for everything you do," she said. "Now, get out of here. You have to get ready for your trip, and Semy and I have a lot to get into."

"You two better behave. I won't be here to bail you out of jail."

Kirby laughed. "Get out of here. Oh wait, you said you wanted to talk to me about something."

Silver looked down and patted the envelope against his palm. "It was nothing," he said, crinkling his nose and shaking his head.

"Okay, get out of here. Enjoy your time off; you deserve it."

CHAPTER TWO

"YOU CAN DROP me off here," Silver said to the driver.

"Yes, sir," the driver said before veering off the busy street and parking near the curb.

"You don't have to wait for me, I'll catch a cab home."

"You sure?"

"Yep. Thanks for chauffeuring me around today," Silver said as he stepped out of the car and onto a foot-traffic heavy sidewalk.

The driver pulled off and Silver stretched under a dusk-filled sky before directing his attention to a unit with the words *McLarens' Sports Bar* printed above it. Silver smiled as he entered but crinkled his nose at the smell of alcohol and chicken wings. Blaring music stuffed the bar, and every ten seconds, a new customer entered.

He looked behind the bar counter and spotted his favorite bartender and friend, Julia. She was on the opposite side, serving drinks to a group of rowdy men. Silver found a stool and watched as Julia placed a line of shots in front of the men. They downed the drinks, then threw their arms in the air and screamed like they were at a Super Bowl game.

Silver grinned and shook his head before looking at Julia again. She wore a pair of fitted blue jeans and a black long-sleeve button-up shirt with her hair tied back. She looked good. After a few seconds, she looked Silver's way, and a smile grew on her face as she walked to him.

"Why hello there, Mr. Silver," she said.

"I thought you'll be done by now."

"Oh, I am. Just helping out a little, Fridays can get crazy."

Silver nodded and smiled. "So. Are you ready for this?"

Julia's eyes and mouth both widened. "Am I! This trip's all I've been thinking about today, all I've been thinking about this week." She smiled, eyes still wide.

"Yeah, me too."

The counter vibrated as one of the men on the opposite end began slapping the top.

"Another round," he said before looking at the ceiling and howling.

"I have to take care of this pack of wolves, and after, I'll be ready to go, okay?" Julia said.

Silver chuckled. "I'll be here."

"Do you want anything to drink while you wait?"

"Yeah, give me a Roy Rogers."

"Are you serious? Wait, that's right, you're cutting back."

Silver smiled at her.

"One Roy Rogers coming up," she said as she grabbed a bottle from the shelf, walked to the other side of the bar, and filled the shot glasses for the wolves. On her way back, she replaced the bottle and grabbed a glass and a can of Coke. She sat the glass in front of Silver and poured the Coke before reaching for a bottle of grenadine syrup and adding it to the Coke.

"Here you go," she said while adding a straw and stirring

the drink, then pushing the glass closer to him. "It's on the house."

"Thanks."

Julia placed her elbows on the bar top and rested her chin on her palms. "You're welcome," she said, smiling and looking at him.

Silver took a sip. "Not bad."

Julia pushed from the counter. "Not bad," she said as she rolled her eyes.

"No, it's actually pretty good. The best Roy Rogers I've ever had."

Julia slapped the countertop. "That's more like it."

Silver laughed before taking another sip of his drink.

"While you have your drink, I'll go get my things."

He raised his glass to her as she walked away and disappeared through a set of swinging doors. Five minutes later, Silver finished his drink, and Julia walked from behind the bar with a suitcase, a small duffel bag, and her purse. He grabbed the suitcase and rolled it behind himself as he followed her outside.

"I see you're already packed," Silver said.

"I figured we can just go straight to the airport from your house. I know you don't mind me crashing there."

"How do you know? I could be expecting company."

Julia laughed. "You're not, except for me now."

The two walked to the curb to hail a cab, and fifteen minutes later, they were standing in Silver's apartment.

Julia placed her luggage by the door. "Is this new furniture, Lee?" she said with a big smile as she walked to the living room and rubbed the sofa cushion.

"Yeah, I thought it was time."

"You did the decorations yourself?"

"Yep."

"Why didn't I know about this?"

"Because you haven't been here in almost a week."

Julia performed a ballet spin and plopped on the sofa. "Kirby must be paying you well. Wait, you're not giving her any overtime, are you?"

Silver, still standing, chuckled. "I'm ignoring that question, but she did give me a huge bonus today."

"Really?"

"Yeah, between my pension from my previous job, the money I've made working for her, and the bonus I got today, I'm pretty much set with my finances."

"That reminds me, did you tell her?"

"No, not yet."

"Does she at least know about you—you know, being James Bond and all."

"You mean does she know I used to be an assassin for the government. I think she may know something, but I never shared any details."

Julia hunched her shoulders. "Well, what makes you think she knows anything?"

"Kirby may be young, but she's very well connected. When she first asked me about the ten-year gap in my portfolio, I just told her it was classified. But I don't think she would've kept me around this long without doing a little more digging into me and being okay with what she found, so I'm not too concerned about it either way."

Julia rested her elbow on the back of the sofa, tracked her hand through her hair, and massaged the back of her head. "That's fine, but you still should tell her your plans."

"I will. Just haven't gotten around to it."

Julia yawned. "Okay, well, we have to get up early and

I'm hungry. Let's order pizza, my treat. No, better yet, your treat."

Silver smiled. "That's a great idea."

Early the next morning, Silver rose from the sofa and stretched before walking to his bedroom and knocking on the door. After a few seconds, he heard movement and a moan from the other side.

"Ahh, is it time to go already?" Julia said.

"Yeah, we need to be at the airport in two hours."

It took them an hour and a half to clean up, dress, get to LaGuardia, go through security, and make it to their gate. Their plane just started boarding when they arrived, and they were among the first to board and take their seats since they were in first class. Julia sat by the window and Silver sat next to her in the aisle seat. The next twenty minutes were noisy, with passengers entering and stowing their luggage and the flight attendants giving directions. Twenty minutes after that, the plane was in the air and the flight attendant served breakfast. It was sausage, eggs, hash browns, toast, fruit, and juice. Silver had orange juice with his breakfast, and Julia had apple juice with hers. The two talked and napped for six hours before landing in Denver.

"The first leg's over," Sliver said as the plane parked at the jetway.

"I don't know if I can handle another six hours, Lee," Julia said.

"Sure you can. Think about the beach and palm trees."

She lifted her chin and raised an eyebrow. "Okay, you're right. I can."

The intercom scratched, and the flight attendant's voice

spoke. "In a few moments the cabin door will open. We ask that you remain seated until the overhead seatbelt light is off. If this is your final destination, we want to thank you for flying with us and wish you a great stay here in Denver, Colorado. And for those who will continue with us to Honolulu, we ask that you remain seated while others deplane. We'll be around shortly to serve refreshments."

A moment later, the flight attendant pulled the cabin door latch until the door thumped and hissed open. A ding permeated the cabin and the clicking of seat belts followed. Over half the passengers stood, gathered their belongings, and herded off the plane and into the jet bridge. When the aisle cleared, Silver stood, stretched, then went to the restroom. On his way back, he found Julia in the aisle, stretching her hands above her head.

"I'm going to the restroom," she said as she slid past him.

Silver nodded and then took his seat.

Shortly after, three people entered the plane. Two were Asian men. Both dressed in jeans and light coats. The first guy had a clean shave and wore his hair tapered, while his partner sported a bald head and goatee. A woman in handcuffs walked between the two. She wore jeans with a short-sleeved shirt and had long, dark hair, full lips, and a heart-shaped face. She looked Asian but more Pacific Islander, given her light brown complexion. As the group passed through the aisle, Silver saw a badge and gun on one of the man's hips. *U.S. Marshals.* The three continued up the walkway until they found their seats near the back of the plane.

Julia exited the restroom and walked back to her seat. Silver stood, and she scooted past him to the window.

"Did I miss anything?" Julia asked as she sat.

Silver shook his head. "Nope."

Six and a half hours later, the plane landed at The Daniel K. Inouye International Airport, and Silver and Julia were the first off the aircraft. They threaded through the airport and made it to ground transportation, where they found their shuttle service. Moments later, they climbed into the back seat of a small van and left the airport. Sunlight penetrated through the partly clouded afternoon sky and shone over various bodies of water and mountains in the distance.

"Ahh, it's so beautiful here, Lee," Julia said as she fixated on the passenger side window.

"It's definitely a sight."

"I know you've come here before, but how many times?"

"A few."

"For work?"

Silver shrugged.

"Oh, I get it, it's *classified*," Julia said.

Silver looked at her and smiled.

The van droned down the road a few more miles and palm trees and buildings rolled by as they drove through downtown Honolulu. Silver and Julia continued to take in the sights until the driver turned into a driveway with tall palms on either side. The driver continued until they arrived at the front of a large resort.

"We're here," he said before throwing the van in park, sliding out, and opening the van's trunk.

When Silver exited the shuttle, the driver held his luggage, which was only a small duffel bag.

"That's mine, I'll carry it," Silver said to the driver as he grabbed the bag.

"I see you like to pack light," the driver said.

"Take only what you need; more than that is just extra weight."

"I hear that, makes my job a lot easier at least. I'll get the rest from the back."

When Julia stepped out of the van, she walked with Silver into the resort while the driver followed closely behind with her luggage. They went to the receptionist desk, tipped the shuttle driver, checked in, then took the elevator upstairs to their adjoining rooms. Both had their own bathroom, living area, and bed. Silver and Julia figured it was best for them to have a little privacy. At least that's what they agreed on.

Silver tossed his bag on the bed before walking to the balcony window and sliding the blinds open. Light raced in, warming his face, and a view spanning from the beach and out into the ocean came into sight. He took it all in for a moment before hearing a knock from the room's adjoining door. Julia stood on the other side with a big smile.

"I love it here!" she said while brushing past him and into his room. "The floors are marble, I have a king-size bed, a rain shower, and a jacuzzi. What's in your bathroom?" she asked as she darted toward his bathroom.

"The same as your room."

While Julia was in Silver's bathroom, he took a seat on the couch in the living area.

"Oh, yours has the same setup as mine," Julia said from the bathroom.

"Yeah, I told you that."

She walked into the living room. "Oh wow, look at that view," she said, continuing toward the balcony window. "This is amazing, Lee!"

Silver watched as she peered out the balcony window and swayed from side to side like a cheerful kid looking outside at falling snow on Christmas morning. She remained that way for thirty seconds before skipping across the marble floor to his bed and diving onto it. She lay on her side with her elbow pressed into the bed and her head resting in her palm.

Silver stood and walked to her.

"So, what do you want to do first?" she asked.

"We can do whatever you like."

Julia stared at him for a moment before sitting up and standing. "Thank you so much for this," she said, hugging him. "I've pretty much never taken a true vacation and really needed this."

Silver hugged her back. "I have to take care of my favorite bartender, especially since you've always been there for me when I've needed it."

She squeezed him harder, and after a long moment, the two slowly loosened their embrace but still held one another. They looked into each other's eyes and both gradually leaned in to kissing distance.

A loud thump came from the side of the bed. They released each other and saw Silver's bag on the floor.

"Sorry, I must've knocked it to the edge when I jumped on your bed," Julia said.

They laughed.

"So, let's get out of here and get this vacation rolling," Silver said.

"Yes! Let's start with walking on the beach and spending some time by the pool."

"Sounds good to me."

Twenty minutes later, they were on the beach, walking along the coastline. Silver had changed into shorts and a white t-shirt, and Julia wore a gold-colored swimsuit with a laced white shawl tied around her waist. They trekked across the soft, tan-colored sand in flip-flops as the warm water brushed over their feet and the cool breeze wafted across their faces. People lined the beach. Some lay on towels, some on a beach chair, while others played in and on the sand.

Julia stopped and looked at the horizon.

Silver followed her gaze beyond the swimmers, surfers, canoes, and sailboats. "Quite the sight, huh?"

"Yes, it's absolutely beautiful."

They continued up the beach and walked for over an hour before heading to the pool and having a few virgin daiquiris and pina coladas. While there, the server told them about a restaurant that served the best steak and seafood in town, so they went upstairs, changed clothes, and walked to the restaurant. Silver enjoyed the most tender steak he had in a long time, and Julia raved about the lobster. They ate, talked, and laughed for two hours before heading back to the resort. It was dark when they entered the lobby.

Julia sighed. "That was so much fun," she said as they approached the elevators.

"It was, but I think all the traveling and walking is catching up with me," Silver said before pressing the up arrow.

"Yeah, I'm ready for bed."

When they entered the elevator, Silver jabbed their floor number, but before the doors could close, a familiar man entered. The U.S. Marshal with the tapered haircut. He carried a large brown bag with grease stains at the bottom and a beverage holder with three Styrofoam cups.

"Floor?" Silver asked him.

The man tilted his head and looked at the elevator's control panel. "That's it."

Silver eased toward the back of the elevator with Julia and kept his eye on the guy's back.

"I don't know about you, but I'm going to soak in the jacuzzi," she said.

"I think I'll do the same," Silver said, still looking at the guy.

"Tomorrow we should take a tour."

"Uh huh."

Julia turned to Silver. "Lee, are you even listening to me?"

He looked at her with wrinkles across his forehead. "Of course I am."

The man glanced over his shoulder at them. Shortly after, the elevator dinged, and the doors slid apart. The man stepped out. Silver and Julia followed him all the way to their rooms. While Julia removed her keycard and fiddled with her door, Silver watched the man go to a room at the end of the hall and knock on the door.

Julia pushed her door open. "I'm going to figure out how to work the jacuzzi, then I may be over to bother you, okay?"

Silver didn't answer; he just kept his eyes on the guy.

"Did you hear me?" Julia asked, pivoting toward Silver's gaze.

By that time, the door opened, and the man walked inside.

Julia faced Silver again. "What are you doing?" she asked with a slight chuckle.

"Nothing, I just remember seeing that guy on our plane, that's all."

"Oh, really. Well, it's not uncommon, so did you hear what I say?"

"Yeah, you'll be over to bother me," Silver said, grinning as he did.

"Whatever," Julia said before stepping inside her room and sticking her tongue out at him.

Silver rolled his eyes as the door shut in front of him. He glanced down the hall at the room the man entered. "Probably nothing. I'm here to relax," he said to himself before entering his own room.

CHAPTER THREE

THE NEXT MORNING, Silver woke to knocking from the adjoining door. He opened it to find Julia standing on the other side. She wore a heather-gray t-shirt, twisted into a knot at the bottom, white capri pants, and gray Adidas with white stripes.

"Why are you knocking?" Silver said, as he turned and walked toward the bathroom. "The door's unlocked."

"I didn't want to walk in while you were in your birthday suit," Julia said.

Silver entered the bathroom and washed his face. When he came out, Julia was looking outside through the balcony window.

"I see you're already dressed," he said.

She turned from the window. "Yep. I figured we can get an early start, maybe have some breakfast first."

"Sounds good," Silver replied, as he removed a pair of blue jeans and a polo shirt from his bag.

"Okay," Julia said, before walking to the adjoining door. "I'm going to grab my things while you get ready."

Twenty minutes later, they were in a buffet line at one of

the resort's restaurants. Silver filled his plate, grabbed a bottle of orange juice, and found a place for them to sit. Julia found him a couple of minutes after and set her plate on the table.

"I'll be back, have to run to the restroom," she said.

Silver nodded, chewed his breakfast, and watched as Julia dodged around a few tables before disappearing down a hall. Halfway through his next bite, he noticed two men enter the restaurant. The U.S. Marshals he saw the day before, but they weren't wearing their badges today. The bald one with the goatee held the back of his head, wide eyes, and looking from side to side while his clean shaved partner scanned the room with his mouth gaped. Silver kept his eyes on them as they threaded through the dining area. He wanted to ignore them; he wanted to finish his breakfast and enjoy his time with Julia, but he didn't like being in the dark with a potentially dangerous situation.

"Lost something?" he asked as the two men approached his table.

The bald guy stopped and gave Silver a stare as if he didn't see him sitting there. "I'm looking for a colleague," the man said while reaching into his pocket and removing his phone. He tapped and swiped at it before turning the screen to Silver. "Have you seen this woman?" he asked.

It was a picture of the woman who traveled with them on the plane.

"Who are you?"

"Just a local looking for my colleague."

Silver looked at the gun on the man's hip. "Are you a cop?" he asked.

The man followed his gaze. "Oh no, but I have a permit for this. So, have you seen her?"

Silver took another bite of his food. "I have."

"You have?" the man said before waving to his partner. "Where?"

"On the plane yesterday with you, but I haven't seen her since."

The man scoffed. "Don't waste my time," he said, placing the phone back inside his pocket.

At that moment, the guy with the tapered haircut walked to his bald partner. "What?" he asked.

The bald man shook his head. "Nothing. Let's go."

Silver watched as the two men left the same way they entered. A couple of minutes later, Julia made her way to the table and sat across from him.

"Wow, you just about cleared your plate," she said.

"Yep," Silver replied.

"So, did I miss anything?"

"Nope—well, there is something."

Julia's forehead wrinkled, and she leaned toward Silver with her elbow on the table and her chin in her palm.

"I don't mean to ruin our vacation," Silver said, "but yesterday on the plane, there were two men—"

"You're talking about the men that were with that woman?"

Silver raised an eyebrow. "You noticed them?"

"Yeah, they were sitting near the back of the plane. Don't look so surprised; you're the one always telling me to mind my surroundings."

"No, I'm just shocked you listened to me."

They both chuckled.

"Okay, so what about them?" Julia asked.

"Well, they're staying here."

"They are?"

"You didn't notice the man in the elevator last night?"

"No, I guess I missed that."

"Looks like we have to hone those observation skills."

Julia tilted her head and poked her lip at him.

"But anyway, the two men came in here while you were in the restroom. They were looking for the woman."

"Really?"

"Yeah. It may not be a big deal, but something is going on. Just wanted to make sure you were aware because the two guys are carrying guns."

"Guns? I didn't realize that."

"Um-hum, so if you see them or the woman, stand clear."

"What do you think? I'll go introduce myself to them?" Julia said, as she took the first bite of her breakfast.

"I do recall telling you to stay away from someone before, and you didn't listen. Remember? You had to get out of town."

"That was before I knew you were a secret agent man."

"Right," Silver said, before taking a swig of his orange juice.

"Hey. Do you think we should let the resort's security staff know?"

Silver shrugged. "It won't hurt. That way, it's in the hands of the authorities, and we can enjoy our trip."

They finished their breakfast and made their way to the receptionist in the lobby.

"Good morning, how can I help you?" the young lady at the counter said.

"Good morning. Is there someone from security we can talk to?" Silver asked.

"Is there an issue?"

"I hope not. Just wanted to make them aware of a situation."

"Okay, one moment," she said before entering a room behind the counter.

Julia sighed. "Hopefully this doesn't take too long. I have an exciting day planned."

Silver looked at her and smiled.

A minute later, the receptionist returned. "Someone with security will be down in a few minutes, sir," she said.

Silver nodded. "Appreciate it," he said.

"My pleasure, sir."

Silver then turned to Julia, "While we're waiting for them, I'm going to the bathroom."

"Alrighty, I'll be here, waiting," she said.

Silver went to the restroom and was back in the lobby within four minutes. He saw the receptionist standing next to a man in a black polo shirt and dark khaki green cargo pants with a Ruger LC9 holstered on his hip, but he didn't see Julia.

"This is one of our on-duty officers," the young lady said as Silver approached.

"Hello sir, I understand you had some concerns you wanted to discuss," the man said.

"Yeah," Silver said, while scanning the moderately crowded lobby for Julia. "Where's the woman I was with earlier..." he asked the receptionist as he spotted Julia standing outside near the front entrance.

He stepped in that direction, and while squinting at the glass doors, he saw Julia talking to someone. *The woman from the plane.* Silver increased his walking speed, and as he did, he heard the security officer stepping behind him.

"Sir, sir," the officer called.

Continuing toward the front entrance, Silver glanced back at the officer. When he returned his sights to the front entrance, he saw the two men from the plane hustling out the door and toward the women. Silver sprinted through the lobby, with the security officer following him. As Silver exited the front door, the man with the goatee raised his pistol toward Julia and the Asian woman.

Silver shoulder-butted him, causing the bald man to drop his gun and stumble into his partner. Before the gun could settle on the pavement, Silver scooped it up and aimed it at the two men.

"What do you think you're doing?" he asked them.

Neither of the two men answered, just stood with their arms raised. Julia and the woman with the heart-shaped face watched intently, with gaping mouths and the white of their eyes exposed. Hotel guests and passersby gasped at the sight.

Silver took a step toward the men and said, "Who are—"

"Drop the weapon," the security officer interrupted, with his gun trained on Silver.

Silver watched the officer from his peripheral but kept his gun on the bald man and his clean shaved partner. "These are the two you want to aim your gun at," Silver said to the officer.

"I won't ask again."

Julia and the woman took cover behind a taxicab at the curb, while pedestrians scattered from the area.

Silver looked at the officer, held the gun by the trigger guard with one finger, opened his arms, knelt to the ground, and slid the gun from his finger to the pavement. He then stood with his arms raised and shrugged at the officer.

The security officer kept his gun on Silver. "Good, now kick it over."

As Silver moved his leg to do as the officer asked, he saw the man with the clean shave and tapered hair lifting his own pistol in the security officer's direction.

"Get down!" Silver yelled while diving at guard.

A roaring boom popped through the air, and glass shattered as Silver and the officer crashed through the doors. Silver felt pieces of glass rain down on his back as he and the officer hit the lobby's floor. More people screamed and ran from the lobby and front entrance. Julia and the woman entered the taxicab. The Asian woman jumped in the driver's seat and Julia entered through the back driver's side.

The bald guy picked up his gun. "Let's get her," he said to his partner.

The officer moaned.

Silver inspected his body and saw where the bullet entered his left shoulder.

"You're lucky," Silver told him.

"I don't feel lucky," the officer said.

"Just keep pressure on your shoulder until the medics arrive."

Screeching and gunfire flowed through the air. The cab raced around the resort's driveway and headed for the exit. The two men commandeered a small delivery truck parked near the curb and gave chase.

"You don't mind, do you?" Silver asked the security officer as he picked up the officer's Ruger LC9 and dashed outside into smoke and the scent of burnt rubber.

He ran after the truck and hopped on the back bumper as it slowed to make a right turn onto a six-lane highway. He then braced himself by holding the vertical metal rod of the right-side cargo door. The truck rocked and swayed as it droned down the road. Silver tucked the Ruger in his back waistband and straddled to the left side of the truck. The wind struck his face as he peeked around the corner and saw the taxicab twelve yards ahead. Cars honked as the delivery truck zipped past and crossed in and out of lanes.

Grabbing the outside frame of the door with his free hand and tightening his grip on the metal rod with his other, Silver used his feet and shimmied himself to the roof of the cargo trunk. He lay on his belly and crawled toward the front of the truck as the wind pulled at his shirt. When he was halfway to the truck's cabin, the vehicle jerked to the left, and a loud thump followed. The momentum of the truck slid Silver in that direction and over the edge. With the left side of his body hanging over the edge, he looked down and saw a large dent in the taxicab's front passenger door. In the back seat, Julia sat crouched with her arms covering her head, while the woman driving leaned toward the windshield with both hands on the wheel.

Silver pulled himself back on the delivery truck's roof and snailed his way toward the cabin. Traffic thinned, and the palm trees and buildings rolling by on either side were soon replaced by forestry, large bodies of water, and mountains in the distance. Gripping the edge of the cabin's roof and peeking into the driver's side, Silver thrust his left arm through the half-opened window and grabbed the clean shaved man's throat.

"Pull over!" he yelled.

The man took one hand off the wheel and clasped Silver's arm. "G—get off me," he said, struggling to break Silver's grip.

The truck weaved across the highway, and as Silver felt his body sliding toward the edge again, he released his hold on the man's throat and grasped the inside window frame instead. A car driving in the opposite direction laid on its horn until the delivery truck veered onto the right side of the road.

Silver glanced down and saw the cab right next to the truck, and before he could fully adjust his body on the roof, a blast roared from inside the truck's cabin. He quickly released his grip and slid back toward the trunk as two large bullet holes ripped through the cabin's roof. Holding the front brim of the trunk and removing the Ruger, Silver fired three rounds through the cabin's roof. The truck skidded to the left. Silver tucked the Ruger back inside his pants, held tight with both hands, and watched the taxicab screech to a halt as the delivery truck cut it off and stopped in front of it.

Silver climbed down on the driver's side and lurked toward the front. The door swung open and the man with the tapered haircut hopped out from behind the wheel. The moment the clean-shaved man's feet hit the ground, Silver delivered a punch to his jaw. The guy spun, hit the open door, and then fell to the pavement. Silver removed the Ruger and aimed it at the door before jumping inside the cabin. On the passenger side, the bald guy sat, holding his bleeding shoulder. He eyed Silver, then reached for his gun in the middle of the seat. Silver beat him to it, snatching the gun, ejecting the magazine, then tossing the gun out the door.

The injured man chuckled. "You're a dead man," he said. "Do you know who we work for?"

"No, and I get the feeling you're not going to tell me either, huh?" Silver said.

"That's right, I'm not telling you—"

Silver elbowed the man in the head near his temple. The guy slumped over, knocked out.

"You don't have to tell me now; sleep on it," Silver said as he hopped out of the truck.

By that time, traffic had bottlenecked. Some vehicles stopped and looked at the scene, while others slowed just long enough to thread through and continue on their way. Ignoring the honking horns and fussing drivers, Silver walked to Julia, who stood with the other woman near the hood of the cab.

"You couldn't help yourself, could you?" he said.

Julia shrugged. "What are you talking about?"

Silver pointed at the Asian woman. "Her. I told you to stay away."

"It's not what you think."

"Really? Because it looks like you got involved after I told you to stand clear, and I almost killed myself trying to save you."

"First, you're not my dad, and no one told you to jump on the roof of a truck like Spiderman. Second, she was escaping from those men. She said they were going to hurt her."

"Ah, okay. Thank you for clearing that up. The strange woman says it's okay, so it's okay. There's no chance she could be lying, right?"

"Hey, I can hear you; I'm right over here," the woman said.

Julia scoffed before folding her arms and shaking her head. "I forget you can be over the top sometimes," she said to Silver. "And she has a name, Alleen."

"Oh really? I'm sorry I didn't catch it. I was too busy hanging from the back of a truck," Silver said as he pointed at the delivery truck.

"Excuse me," Alleen said.

Julia ignored her. "You didn't even ask if I was okay," she said to Silver. "You just came over and ridiculed me without getting the whole story."

"We need to go," Alleen said.

"I know you, so I know how the story went," Silver told Julia before turning his attention to Alleen.

"Maybe you don't know me as well as you think," Julia said back to him.

Silver followed Alleen's gaze and saw two black SUVs approaching the delivery truck. "We'll finish this later, but we need to go," he said.

"Where are we going to go?" Julia asked. "We're surrounded by jungle, and the cab is blocked in."

"Follow me," Alleen said before jogging to the edge of the road. She climbed over the guardrail and waved at Silver and Julia. "C'mon."

"What should we do?" Julia asked Silver.

"We're in it now. Let's go," Silver said, placing his hand on Julia's back and guiding her to where Alleen stood. Once he helped Julia over the guardrail, Silver glanced back at the SUVs and saw a group of men armed with assault rifles exiting the vehicles. They didn't look his way, just surrounded the delivery truck, and as they did, a man with shades exited one of the SUVs. His suit was a perfect fit for his athletic built, and his slicked back, salt-and-pepper hair matched the color of his full beard.

Silver stared at the man for a moment before hearing Julia and Alleen's voices.

"We have to go now," Alleen said.

"Lee, let's go," Julia said.

Silver jumped over the guardrail, and the group hiked down a grassy incline, then into the woods.

CHAPTER FOUR

THEY WALKED THROUGH the jungle for nearly an hour with Alleen leading the way. It was humid. Mosquitoes buzzed around them, Birds chirped from the tree branches canopied above them, and critters rattled the shrubs on either side of them.

"We can rest here," Alleen said as she sat on a log.

"Good idea," Julia said, before leaning against a large oak tree.

Silver looked around the area. "Okay, but not for too long. If they're tracking us, it won't take them long to catch up."

Alleen shook her head. "Don't worry about that," she said. "I know this land. I'll circle back and make sure it's difficult for them to track where we're going."

"And exactly where is it we're going?" Silver asked as he approached her.

Alleen, still sitting, looked at him. "It's just on the other side of the mountain," she said, pointing to her right. "We'll be safe there."

"Wait," Julia said. "Why can't we just go back to the resort?"

Silver shook his head. "No. They probably already sent some men to the resort, just in case we went back. And I bet whoever's after you," he looked at Alleen, "is well connected. So, while we have a minute, why don't you tell us who those men are and why they were chasing you."

Alleen looked at the ground. "It's a long story."

"Tell us the important bits."

"Simply put, I've witnessed their criminal operation, and they want to keep me silent."

"What's their operation?"

Alleen stood and sighed. "Murder, drugs, human trafficking, robbery."

Julia walked to Silver and stood next to him while Alleen turned and stepped in the direction of the mountain she had pointed to earlier.

"None of those sound like things you'd approve of," Silver said.

Alleen glanced over her shoulder. "Absolutely not."

"So, how did you get involved?"

Alleen sighed again before turning to face them. "Trust me when I say I had no choice."

Silver chuckled. "Trust you?"

"Lee," Julia said as she nudged her elbow into his side.

"Fine. Why were you in Denver? And why were those two... criminals wearing U.S. Marshal badges?"

"I went to meet an FBI agent who said he could help put this group away and keep us safe," Alleen said. "Agent Brooks was his name. We met at his office. I told him everything I saw and gave him the address for my hotel. He told me to go back there and wait because he'd send some U.S. Marshals to escort me to a more secure location. I waited for a few hours, then those two men you saw me with knocked on the door and told me to come with them. I didn't think too much of it until they entered the room and put me in cuffs."

"Wait-wait-wait. You saw their badges before letting them in?"

"Of course. That's why I let them in."

"Okay, but why didn't you make a scene in the airport, after you knew they were the bad guys?"

"They had guns," Julia said.

"Exactly, I didn't want anyone to get hurt, I guess," Alleen said.

Wrinkles crossed Silver's forehead, but he said nothing.

"But anyway," Alleen continued. "This morning at the resort, they uncuffed me in the room. One went to the bathroom while the other stood in the living area. I grabbed a wooden vase and hit the back of his head as hard as I could before running out of the room. They chased me downstairs, but I hid in a closet on the first floor. I heard them run past, so I waited in the closet for ten more minutes before leaving. I guess it was my nerves; felt they could still be waiting for me right outside of the closet. When I finally left, I ran into Ms. Julia in the lobby. I told her some men were after me, and she walked me outside where we exchanged names and tried to get a cab."

Silver looked at Julia.

She nodded. "I figured it was better to move than to stand there and wait for them to come."

Silver sighed. "Who was the Japanese guy in the suit and shades?" he asked Alleen.

Alleen paused a beat before looking at the ground. "Oh him. His name is Kazan Shima," she said with a hint of disdain in her voice. "He's their leader and has ties to the Yakuza."

"The Yakuza?" Julia said.

Alleen nodded. "Yes. He's been giving us all kinds of problems."

"That's the second time I heard you say *us*," Silver said. "Are there other witnesses besides you?"

"There's a small village of us," Alleen said as she turned to face the mountain once more. "That's where we're going."

"The jungle, Yakuza, and possibly corrupt law enforcement. Not what I had in mind for my vacation."

"I'm so sorry. I can point you in the direction of the resort—or the airport."

"No, he's just being sarcastic," Julia said.

"It's best we stick together," Silver said as he walked to Alleen. "How certain are you that they won't be able to track us?"

"About eighty percent," Alleen said.

Silver puckered his lips before saying, "I'm good with those odds. Let's get moving."

Alleen took the lead, and they continued toward the mountain. The terrain was wet, and the chirping, thrumming, and buzzing were continuous. Julia spotted a couple of deer and then later a mongoose. She was the only one focused on the wildlife. Alleen was familiar with the land, so she had probably seen it all before, and Silver had spent a fair share of time in the wilderness, so he didn't focus on the cute animals. He was too busy keeping an eye out for the dangerous ones.

They walked for what felt like a couple of miles before reaching a twenty-foot-tall waterfall. At the top, the water rolled white before turning clear and falling into a small pond in front of them.

"We can take a break here," Alleen said. "This water is okay to drink."

The three knelt, cupped their hands into the water, and put it to their mouths and across their faces.

Silver saw an opening behind the waterfall. "Is that a cave?" he asked.

Alleen followed his gaze. "Yes, but we're not going that way. We're going around it."

"Why? It seems quicker."

"That way will add unnecessary challenges. Not worth it."

Silver shrugged. "You're the guide," he said as he took another sip of water.

After a few minutes, they stood and hiked uphill toward the waterfall. At the top, on the right, a rushing river ran toward the waterfall. On their left, trees and shrubs formed a wall of greenery. The trail was narrow, only three feet separating the river from the foliage. Alleen continued to navigate with Julia a few paces behind her and Silver last in line. They walked for a quarter of a mile before Julia screamed and slapped at her head. A gecko had leapt from a bush and into her hair.

Alleen turned with the white of her eyes exposed.

"Relax, calm down, I'll get it," Silver said, as he walked toward Julia.

She stumbled to the riverbank's edge, still panicked and focused on the gecko.

"Watch out!" Silver shouted.

Julia tripped and splashed into the racing water. The current swept her back in the opposite direction. Silver sprinted after her, and Alleen was on his heels. They dodged around tree limbs and jumped over fallen branches. Silver picked up speed, creating a sizeable gap between him and Alleen, but the faster he ran, the farther Julia drifted. Her head went under the water then resurfaced, and her arms flapped the entire time. This went on for a long seven seconds before she grabbed hold of a log in the middle of the river. It gave Silver time to catch up to her. He saw her struggling to hold her grip, so he snatched a long tree branch from the ground and extended it to her.

"Grab it!" he said.

Alleen dashed to Silver and held his arm as he stretched across the river with the branch.

Julia reached for it but lost her hold. The current whisked her downstream.

Silver continued after her. She bobbed below and above the surface, and her screams flowed over the crashing water. It was a matter of seconds before they were back at the waterfall. Silver remembered the drop was only about twenty feet, so he felt good about that. What he couldn't remember was if Julia could swim or not. She quickly floated yards ahead of him before disappearing into the water's whitecaps. Silver raced down the hill, threw the Ruger on the ground, and dove into the pond. He looked under the water but didn't see Julia. He rose to the surface and looked, but still didn't see her.

"Jules!"

On his second dive under, he saw movement. When he resurfaced, Julia was in front of him, treading water.

"You okay?" he asked.

"Do I look okay?"

"Are you hurt?"

"No."

"That's good news."

"Why didn't you jump in after me?"

"What?" Silver said, squinting as wrinkles crossed his nose and forehead while he continued to tread water.

"You heard me," Julia said as she swam toward the bank.

As she did, the sound of birds squawking and flapping away in fear wafted through the air. Silver peered through the jungle and saw two of Shima's men approaching the pond. They were fifteen yards away and didn't appear to notice him, Julia, or Alleen.

"Hey-hey," Silver whispered to Julia. "They're here."

Julia paused before slowly back paddling toward Silver.

Silver looked at Alleen, pointed at his eyes, then toward the men. She looked, then nodded. Next, he pointed at the Ruger on the ground and waved for her to come into the water. She nodded again before picking up the gun and tiptoeing into the water. The three softly swam across the pond and behind the waterfall. They crawled into the cave and watched as the two armed men approached the pond.

Silver extended his hand to Alleen, and she handed him the Ruger.

"I thought you said it would be hard for them to track us," he whispered.

"It would've been if we had made it past the river," she replied.

One man stared at the ground. He paused for a few seconds before signaling his partner and giving him the same hand gesture that Silver had given Alleen earlier. The men scanned the ground and then looked toward the waterfall.

"Get down," Silver said, as he dropped to his belly.

Julia and Alleen did the same.

The men then turned their attention back to the ground before walking up the hill and out of sight.

"I guess we're not going that way," Silver said, while lifting himself from the cave floor.

"No, I guess not," Alleen said.

"I'm sorry," Julia said, flapping her wet clothes. "I know this way is longer."

"Don't be sorry. It's actually much faster, but possibly... challenging."

Silver removed the magazine from the Ruger before reinserting it and inspecting the chamber. "We better move," he said.

Alleen led them through the cave. The walls were damp, and the air inside had a musty-earthy scent. Water dripped from above, and sunlight entered from above. They threaded around large, wet stones and through puddles of water. Minutes later, they reached a part of the cave where gallons of water rained down from the ceiling. Silver looked where the water poured in and saw the vibrant blue afternoon sky framed by a circular opening in the cave's ceiling. The water on the cave's floor formed a tiny river that streamed ahead. It continued for a hundred yards before flowing into a small pool of water. A beam of light shone at the center of the green-blue water.

"Wow, a lake inside of a cave," Julia said. "It feels so majestic."

Alleen smiled. "It's definitely a sight. We'll go around here," she said, pointing at the ledge of the cave's wall. "Be careful," she continued before stepping on the ledge and straddling across.

"Yeah, please be careful," Silver said to Julia. "I don't want to go for another swim."

"Shut up, Lee, it's not even that deep," she said. "I can see the rocks at the bottom."

Once on the other side, they walked a quarter of a mile before a bright light radiated at the far end of the cave.

"We're almost there," Alleen said.

When they exited the cave, the sunlight struck Silver's eyes. It stung. He placed his hand in front of his face while his eyes adjusted. Julia and Alleen did the same. On either side of them were shrubs and palms, but a small, open field sat ten yards ahead. The group walked to the edge of the jungle, where Alleen stopped, narrowed her eyes, and looked around the open field. Julia, standing behind her, pointed across the field.

"There's the mountain. We're close," she said.

Silver stepped up behind Julia. "Yeah, closer, maybe about three miles away. Let's go," he said.

Alleen stuck her arm out.

"What's the matter?" Silver asked.

"Nothing, but we'll have to walk along the perimeter of the field," she said.

"If it's nothing, why can't we just cut across?"

"Please, trust me," Alleen said before pivoting left and walking toward the edge of the jungle.

Silver sighed. "There you go, asking me to trust you again," he uttered to himself.

They continued along the edge until they reached the jungle on the opposite side. Shrubs and trees again encompassed them. One particular tree caught Silver's eye.

"Is that a mango tree?" he asked Alleen.

She followed his gaze. "Yes, it is."

"Good, I can use a snack," Julia said.

Silver pulled one of the tree's branches, and there were seven orange, ripe mangoes hanging from it. He snapped two from the branch, tossing one to Julia and the other to Alleen before yanking one for himself.

"So, how much longer is it?" Julia asked with a mouth full of mango.

"Two hours, maybe a little longer," Alleen answered.

Silver took a bite from his mango before looking at Alleen. "You said this way would be challenging, but so far things have been cool. Can we expect trouble during those hours?"

Alleen hunched her shoulders. "I—I guess it's not as bad as I remembered."

"Right."

"Well, we better keep moving."

"Sure."

After another ten minutes of walking, they reached a small wooden bridge arching over a canal. As soon as they made it across, Silver heard twigs snap and bushes rattle. A man armed with an AK-47 appeared on his right, aiming the gun at the group. Silver stepped toward the man but paused when he saw another armed man approach on the left.

"Hands up!" the man said.

Julia and Alleen immediately raised their hands.

Silver looked at the man to his right.

The man aimed the gun at Silver's head. "Don't think about it, bruddah," he said before removing the Ruger stuffed in the back of Silver's pants and tucking it in the front of his own pants. "Hands up."

Silver slowly raised his arms. "More friends of yours?" he said to Alleen.

A third man approached from the green underbrush. His midsection was chubby, his face round, and his hair buzzed. He walked directly to Alleen and smiled.

"It's been a long time, Alleen," he said.

CHAPTER FIVE

ALLEEN FROWNED AND turned her face from the chubby man.

"What? You have nothing to say to me?" he asked.

Alleen said nothing.

"Fine, let's get them to the village," the man said before grabbing Alleen's arm and pulling her along.

She yanked her arm from him.

"You can either come along willingly, or I'll drag you."

Alleen squinted her eyes and crinkled her nose but said nothing.

"Fine, tie their hands."

One of the armed men removed zip ties from his pocket while the other kept his gun trained on Silver, Julia, and Alleen. The man with the zip ties, then secured their hands behind their backs before raising his rifle at them again.

The chubby man gripped Alleen's arm and guided her into the thicket. Silver and Julia followed with AK-47s aimed at their backs. The group trekked through the shrubbery until they reached a dirt road. Fifty yards up the road, two black jeeps waited for them, with two more men armed with

AK-47s. They put Alleen in the first jeep with the chubby guy and two armed men, while Silver and Julia were put in the second jeep with the other two men. They drove half a mile, then veered off the road onto a bumpy, muddy pathway, before driving another mile and arriving at a seven-foot-tall wooden gate. A woman and a man stood at the gate with rifles strapped over their shoulders. As the first jeep approached, the man and woman opened the gate and waved them through.

On the other side of the gate was a green plot of land with five rectangular-shaped modular homes spread across it. The homes were wooden and wore a fresh glossy finish. They had open breezeways, large windows, lights, and solar-paneled roofs. As the jeeps pulled in, a group of children chased behind them, smiling and laughing before turning away and running toward a hut with a pili grass roof. The jeeps snaked through the village and smoke with the stench of pork wafted in the air. Silver saw more huts and noticed at least four different armed men as they drove towards a small hangar in an open field. Beyond the hangar, and perimeter of the village, were the mountains.

The jeeps parked near the hangar and one of the armed men from Silver's jeep hopped out.

"Get out," the man said with his hand on his rifle.

Silver and Julia slid out of the jeep. They then stood and watched as the chubby guy guided Alleen out of the other jeep. She shrugged her shoulder and twisted her body to break his hold. He pulled her along as he entered the hangar, and Silver and Julia followed with a rifle trained on them. Inside, the hangar was dim, and the air was cool with a hint of gasoline fumes. Silver looked around and saw three fuel drums in the far west corner of the hangar. Shelves, workbenches, and tools filled most of the hangar. But at the center stood a metal pillar with individual chained shackles welded to it.

The chubby man glanced at the pillar, then nodded to one of his men.

The man returned the nod and grabbed Alleen by the arm. "Over here," he said as he walked her to the pillar.

He then cut her zip tie and cuffed her hands with a pair of shackles. The other three armed men cradled their rifles and watched as he did the same to Silver and Julia.

The chubby guy walked to Alleen and shook his head. He stared at her for a long moment before smiling.

"I'll be back; don't go anywhere," he said.

Alleen glared at him as he exited the hangar with his men. The door shut, then clunked before a thump echoed through the hangar.

Silver, Julia, and Alleen all stood quietly around the pillar for a minute before anyone spoke.

"This isn't good," Julia said.

"You should start talking, now," Silver told Alleen.

"It's not as bad as it looks," she said.

"What do you mean?"

"Yeah, Alleen, this is pretty bad," Julia said.

Alleen shook her head. "They're not going to hurt us."

"And how can you be so sure?" Silver said.

"I know them."

"We see that. So, who's that guy?"

Alleen sucked in her lips and glanced at the floor.

"Look, we already have the Yakuza after us, and now this. It's not the time to be tight-lipped."

"His name is Polunu, and he's my cousin."

"Huh?" Julia gasped.

"Excuse me—did you say your cousin?" Silver said.

Alleen nodded.

"Then why are we shackled?"

"We're family, but we've been feuding for some years now. They used to live with us on the other side of the mountain until there was... a situation."

"What kind of situation?"

"Let's just call it a family disagreement. It split up the village, and half moved over here while the other half remained on the other side."

"What was the disagreement about?" Julia asked.

Alleen ignored the question. "I tried to fix it, but here we are."

"Fix it how?"

Alleen didn't answer, just looked at the floor.

"Alleen!"

"Save your breath, Jules," Silver said. "She's not ready to answer, and we need to focus our energy on finding a way out."

Alleen sighed. "I'm sorry for getting you involved in this."

"Don't be sorry, help us find a way out."

Silver inspected the shackle on his right wrist and noticed a small hole where the shackle locked. It was the same on the left shackle. As he scanned around the hangar, he spotted a thin nail on the floor. The chain was too short for him to reach it with his hands, so he stretched his leg out and pulled the nail closer.

"What are you doing, Lee?" Julia asked.

Alleen looked at him but said nothing.

"I'm working on getting us out of here," he said.

He dragged the nail closer until it rolled into the heel of his other foot. He picked it up, inserted it into the shackle hole, and jiggled it around until the shackle snapped opened.

"You got it?" Julia asked.

"Yeah," Silver said as he worked on the shackle around his other wrist.

Once he unlocked it, Sliver went to Julia and did the same to her shackles before going to Alleen and staring at her.

"Am I going to regret this?" he asked her.

She didn't answer.

"Lee," Julia said.

He unlocked Alleen's shackles, and the three walked to the door. Silver opened the door a crack and peeked. The chubby guy, Polunu, was quickly approaching the door with an armed guard. Silver waved for Julia and Alleen to move away. The two women ducked behind the door and placed their backs against the wall. Silver followed them and knelt in front of the women. When the door swung open, Polunu immediately entered with the guard right behind him. There was a pause, then Polunu darted to the metal pillar while the guard surveyed the hangar. Before the door completely shut, Silver pounced on the guard, connecting his fist to the armed man's face. The guard and his rifle fell to the floor. Silver scooped up the AK-47 and aimed it at Polunu, who stood by the metal pillar.

"How about we lock you up, now?" Silver said.

Polunu raised his arms but said nothing.

Alleen walked to Silver, placed her hand on the barrel of the rifle, and lowered it. "No—no, need for that. Unlike some people, I'll never treat my family like an animal without first hearing them out," she said, looking at Polunu.

Polunu looked away, saying nothing.

"Where's Auntie Malie?" Alleen asked him.

"Why?" he asked back.

"Because I need to talk to her. We were working on fixing things."

"Fix it, how? Our family is broken."

"It's not my fault."

"But it's your ohana's fault."

"No. The only family I have lives on both sides of this mountain. You're my family."

Polunu drew in a breath before slowly releasing it.

"Take me to her, please."

Julia peeked out the door. "Guys, we have company."

"Stand back," Silver said, pointing the rifle at the door.

Julia ran behind him.

Alleen fixed on her cousin's face, and he finally made eye contact with her and nodded. By that time, two armed guards stormed in with their rifles aimed at Silver, who had his gun trained on them. The guards barked orders, but Polunu pushed his palms to the men.

"Lower your weapons," he said.

Silver kept his gun on them until they lowered theirs.

"Follow me," Polunu said to Alleen as he walked toward the door.

The man Silver knocked down earlier was getting off the floor. Silver ejected the rifle's magazine, cleared the bullet from the chamber, and handed the gun and magazine to the man. "Sorry about earlier," he said while exiting the hangar with the rest of the group.

Polunu led them to the far east side of the village. They walked past more playing kids, and gardens consisting of radish, lettuce, collard greens, pigeon beans, pineapples, and papaya trees before ending at a large modular home. Silver, Julia, and Alleen followed Polunu inside the house and into a living area. The living room opened into the dining area and kitchen. A full-figured woman with long, dark, gray-streaked hair stood over a steaming stove, and the scent of collard greens and fish filled the air. Polunu walked into the kitchen and patted the woman on her back. She turned to him and listened as he whispered something in her ear. The woman turned to the living room. She and Alleen locked eyes, and both smiled. They walked closer and held hands.

"Are you okay?" the full-figured woman asked Alleen.

Alleen cut her eyes at Polunu. "Yes, Auntie Malie, I'm okay now."

"Who are they?" Malie asked, looking at Silver and Julia.

"They're... they're my friends. Julia and Mr. Silver."

"Welcome," Malie said with a nod.

"Thank you," Silver nodded back.

"This is a lovely home you have," Julia said.

Malie turned her attention back to Alleen. "How did everything go?" she said, before crinkling her nose.

"I ran into some trouble and—" Alleen started.

"Okay-okay, tell me over dinner, after you all wash up. You stink."

An hour later, under the sunset, Silver finished bathing himself using a private outdoor trough near the house. Julia and Alleen had bathed before him and went back inside. He shrugged into a pair of cargo pants and denim shirt Polunu had given him. On his way back inside, he ran into a young lady near the steps.

"I'll take those," she said while extending her arms.

It took Silver a couple of seconds before he realized she was talking about the dirty clothes he carried. "Oh, sorry, thank you," he said as he handed her his clothes.

Inside the house, Malie was still in the kitchen near the stove, and Julia and Alleen were sitting on a couch in the living area, talking. Both wore a muumuu dress. Silver glanced around the house for Polunu, but he was nowhere in sight.

Alleen noticed him. "Everything's okay?" she asked.

"Yeah," Silver said, as he sat in a chair across from the two ladies.

"Where's Polunu?"

"Went to go check on a truck or something. Said he'll be back," Alleen answered. "Well, I'm going to see if Auntie Malie needs any help," she finished before standing and walking to the kitchen.

Silver took in a breath, then exhaled as he reclined in the chair.

"You okay?" Julia asked.

"This has been quite the day."

"Yeah, but it's not all bad. Oh yeah, here," she said, removing a glass of orange-yellow liquid from the end table next to her and handing it to him.

"What is it?"

"It's mango juice. It's really good."

Silver sniffed it. "It smells good," he said before taking a sip. "Mmm, that is good."

"I told you."

Silver pointed to the end table; it had both their phones and his wallet on it. "Has my phone dried yet?"

Julia followed his finger and shook her head. "No, I don't think so."

"I don't know why it's not turning on. It's supposed to be waterproof."

"Mine too, but they took a lot of water."

"That's true."

"I removed the batteries so they could air out. Hopefully they'll start working again once everything dries."

Silver nodded before taking another sip of his juice, and as he did, Julia leaned forward.

"So, what's our plan?" she whispered.

Silver sat up in the chair and shrugged. "Have dinner."

"I know that, but what's the plan afterward?"

"Oh—so now we want a plan. I had one earlier when I told you not to approach her, remember?"

"Not this again."

"Look, you're going to have to trust me and follow my lead, okay?"

Julia nodded. "Yes," she said with a sigh.

"Right now, let's just eat and rest up and gather more information about what's going on, then we can better determine where to go from there."

"Okay."

"You sound worried."

"I am a little. You're used to things like this, but I'm not."

"You know I won't let anything happen to you, right?"

"I know."

"Good," Silver said, leaning in his chair and taking another swig of his juice.

"And Lee."

"Yeah."

"I know you really needed this vacation. I'm sorry it turned out this way."

"Are you kidding me, I'm having a blast," he said with a smile.

Julia chuckled.

In the dining room, plates and silverware knocked and clinked against the tabletop.

Julia peeked over. "Need help setting the table?" she asked Alleen.

Alleen glanced at her, "Sure."

Julia walked into the dining room, and ten minutes later, the four of them were sitting at the table with collard greens, fish, potatoes, and rolls in front of them. Silver and Julia sat next to each other on one side of the table. Alleen sat across from them while Malie sat at the end. Everyone was well into their meals before Malie spoke.

"How is it?" she asked Silver and Julia.

With a mouth full of food, Julia raised her thumb and nodded.

"Everything's great, and this juice is some of the best I've ever had," Silver said.

"Good, happy you're enjoying your meals," Malie said. "Those specific mangoes are from the southwest portion of the island, near Waialae-Kahala."

"Waialae-Kahala, we may have to make a pit stop there."

Malie smiled at him before turning to Alleen. "You said you ran into trouble on the trip. What happened?" she asked.

"I met with that FBI agent, Agent Brooks—"

"Jacob?"

"Yes, Jacob Brooks. We met, and I told him all the bad things I saw the Yakuza do and that there were others who had witnessed their crimes too. Agent Brooks said they're really bad people, and he believed we had enough to build a case against them. He told me to go back to my hotel and wait. He said he was sending U.S. Marshals to take me to a secure location, but the men who showed up were Yakuza."

Malie squinted, and wrinkles crossed her forehead. "Huh... Jacob seemed like a really nice man when I spoke with him. You don't think he's involved with the Yakuza, do you?"

"I'm not sure, Auntie."

At that moment, Polunu entered the house. He stood near the door and stared at the table for a few seconds before walking toward the dining area.

"Food's ready, wasn't sure when you'd get back," Malie said.

"Alright, let me wash up," Polunu said, walking past the dining room. He locked eyes with Silver before disappearing down the hall.

Malie turned her attention to Alleen. "The Yakuza are in many people's pockets, but we did research on Jacob, and he checked out," she said before raising a fork of collards to her mouth. She chewed and shook her head for a minute before dropping her fork on her plate. "I just want these rats out of our land," she blurted.

"I know, Auntie. We may need to come up with something different."

Silver and Julia looked at each other, both chewing. When Silver swallowed his food, he washed it down with his juice and then addressed Malie.

"Do you have a phone here?" he asked.

"Yes, internet too," Malie said as she picked up her fork and jabbed it into her fish.

"If you don't mind, after dinner I'll need to use it."

"No problem."

Polunu strolled into the dining room and sat at the head, opposite Malie, before heaping food onto his plate. "So, what did I miss?"

"We were just talking about how we may need a new plan," Malie said.

"Okay, maybe you can include me on this one."

"Don't start, Polunu," Malie said before, looking in Silver's and Julia's direction. "So, what are your plans?"

Julia didn't speak, just looked at Silver.

"Well, it's a complicated situation," he said. "I'd like to go back to our resort, but that wouldn't be smart right now."

"That's the truth," Polunu said.

"What's that supposed to mean, Polunu?" Alleen asked.

"I have ears on this island. One of my guys heard that Shima and his men are not happy about that stunt this morning on the highway. Word is, he's looking for all three of you."

CHAPTER SIX

THE TABLE WENT silent. Alleen glanced at Silver and Julia, and then her gaze dropped to the table. It was obvious she was in her thoughts. Julia's eyes wandered around the table before stopping on Silver. He shrugged as if he wasn't surprised by Polunu's comment.

"Don't worry," Malie said. "You're all safe here."

"Yeah, don't be scared," Polunu said, looking at Silver and grinning.

Silver stared back. "Do I look scared?" he said with a smirk.

Polunu's smile turned straight, and he placed his attention back on his dinner.

"Where's your phone?" Silver asked Malie.

"Oh, it's right here in the hall," she said, reclining in the chair and pointing in its direction.

"Thank you. Excuse me," Silver said, as he stood from the table and walked toward the hall.

The hall was wide, and there were pictures hanging of Malie and Polunu with people who Silver assumed were family. One picture had Alleen and Malie. In the picture, a woman with short curly hair stood between them and the three were hugged up with big smiles. Silver spotted a cordless phone sitting on top of a console table next to the bathroom door. He picked up the phone and caught a scent of lavender fuming from the bathroom as he dialed a number. The phone rang once, twice, three times, and on the fourth, a giggling woman's voice jumped on the line.

"Hello," she said.

"Hi Semy, it's Silver. Are you two staying out of trouble?"

"Leroy, what's up? We're behaving so far. How's the trip? Are you staying out of trouble?"

"Complicated and unfortunately no."

"That doesn't sound good."

"It's not. At Kirby's house, I saw you had your laptop. Can you look into a few things for me?"

Semy exhaled. "We're all supposed to be on vacation."

"I know, but this is serious, can't wait."

Semy was quiet for a beat. "Are you okay? Is Julia okay?"

"Yeah, we're fine. But I need you to look into the name Kazan Shima—"

"Wait, let me write it down."

"Sure."

Silver held on the line while shuffling and static entered his ear. Seconds later, Semy's voice came through.

"Okay, you said Kazan Shima?" she asked.

"Yes. He's involved with the Yakuza."

"The Yakuza."

"Yes."

"Leroy Silver, what have you gotten yourself into?"

"Not exactly sure, just crossed paths with the wrong people, I guess. Need you to find out all you can on him."

"Okay."

"Also, look into the name Jacob Brooks. He's with the

FBI. I want to know more about him and if he has any association with Shima."

"Sure thing, anything else you need?"

"No, but just to let you know my cell phone is drying out, so if you can't reach me, that may be why. If you can shoot me an email along with the call, that'd help."

"Got it."

"Thanks Semy, I owe you one."

"Well, if we're counting, you actually owe me like two or three."

"You're right."

"But anytime. And Silver."

"Yeah."

"Please be careful."

"You know me."

"That's what I'm afraid of, bye."

"Talk with you later."

Silver ended the call and walked back to the dining room. Julia, Alleen, and Malie were all getting up from the table with their plates in hand. Julia grabbed Silver's plate too, as the three women walked toward the kitchen. Polunu remained at the table, eating his dinner. Silver continued into the living room and out the door. Outside was dark, but the sky was clear, and the moonlight illuminated the village. He walked down the steps and made it ten feet from the house before he heard the door open and close.

"Hey, Lee," Julia said as she trotted to him. "What are you doing?" she asked with a smile.

Silver looked at the sky. "Just getting some air and enjoying the night."

Julia stood next to him and followed his gaze. "Yeah, it's a beautiful night."

They stayed that way for a long moment before Silver caught Julia glancing at him.

"What?" he said.

"Things are getting... dicey, so if something—"

"I told you, I'm not going to let anything happen to you."

"I know, I know, but in the off chance—I—I just want you to know I'm happy we met, and I'm happy I came on this trip with you."

Silver smiled, placed his arm over her shoulder, and pulled her in for a side hug. They looked up at the sky together, then faced one another. The two smiled and chuckled before staring into each other's eyes and slowly closing the distance between their faces. When they were within kissing distance, the door creaked open. They broke their side embrace and put a few inches between them as the door thumped closed.

"Hey, what are you guys up to?" Alleen's voice called from behind them.

"Just out here enjoying the night," Silver said.

"Nothing, it's a beautiful night to be out," Julia quickly followed up.

Alleen walked to them and stood next to Silver. "Yes, it is a lovely night," she said, smiling as she gazed at the sky. This went on for a minute before she turned to face Silver and Julia. "I want you two to know I'm so sorry I got you involved with this. When we get to my village, I'll organize a way for you to get home."

"Alleen, it's okay," Julia said.

"We have some people I trust. They'll get you to the airport safely."

"That's great!"

"Sounds like a plan," Silver said, although he was thinking something different. He knew that even if they got off the island and made it home, Shima had enough resources and pull to pursue them. Going through life while looking over your shoulder was something he had grown accustomed to, but it wasn't something Julia could sustain. He didn't want that kind of life for her, so Silver knew he would have to finish this.

A bright red-orange hue coming from the center of the village caught Silver's eye.

"What's that?" Julia asked.

"Oh, that's probably dancers practicing for the upcoming Aloha Festival," Alleen said.

"So even with all that's going on with the Yakuza, they still hold festivals?" Silver asked.

"We can't stop living."

Silver nodded.

The house door opened and shut once again. This time, Polunu exited with Malie directly behind him.

"Let's go see the dancers," Malie said as they walked past.

Alleen followed them, and Silver and Julia followed her. Music, smoke, and a whiff of charred wood circulated in the air as the group walked to the village's center, where a crowd of people surrounded a burning flame. Some were dancing while others played drums, ukuleles, and flutes. Silver and the group found a seat facing the festivities, and with a view of the mountain in the distance. Silver looked at Julia and saw her smiling. From a seated position, she did her best to mimic the hula dancers by throwing her hands in the air and swaying her hips from side to side. Alleen noticed and laughed before doing the same. Malie had a big smile on her face and Polunu chuckled and shook his head. Once all the dancing and playing stopped, everyone clapped and hooted.

"That was good," Julia said.

"Yeah, it was," Silver agreed.

At that, a teenage boy approached the group and extended his hand to Julia and Alleen.

"We need a few volunteers for hula girls," he said.

Alleen was a little reluctant, but Malie encouraged her to go with a pat on the back, and Julia looked at Silver.

"You should go. Sounds like fun," he said.

"Why not? What the heck," she said, standing and following Alleen and the young man.

They took a few steps before the teenager turned back. "Oh yeah, we need a few fire twirlers too," he said, while sharing his gaze between Silver and Polunu.

"No thanks, I have no experience with that," Silver said.

Polunu shook his head, then hunched his shoulders. It was a gesture that showed he wanted to decline, but Malie told him to go, and Julia and Alleen waved him on.

Polunu grunted. "Ah, fine," he said before standing and following the two ladies and the teenager.

"You guys have fun. I'll stay here with Malie," Silver said, as the three followed the young man to a hut on the opposite side of the fire.

"That's a good kid, you know?" Malie said.

"Who, Alleen or Polunu?" Silver asked.

"Well, both, but I was talking about Alleen. Polunu is a good kid too, he's just passionate and hotheaded."

"I'll say."

"Don't be too hard on him," Malie said with a chuckle. "He had a rough upbringing. You know, I helped raise them both, him and Alleen. They had it tough, especially Polunu. His father is my brother, but him and his wife passed away in a terrible accident."

"I'm sorry."

Malie shook her head. "Thank you, but no need to be sorry, that happened a long time ago. I'm just happy Polunu turned out okay. I know sometimes he can be difficult, but he means well. The same with Alleen, she's difficult but in a different way. She feels she has to carry the weight of the world on her shoulders, alone. She's so much like her mother."

"Her mother's your sister?"

"Yes. Unfortunately, she died too, due to a... a very sad and horrible situation."

Silver shook his head. "I'm so sorry."

Malie cleared her throat. "Thank you. She was a very special person, just like Alleen. I often call it bittersweet. It's bitter because I lost my siblings, but sweet because I had the opportunity to grow closer to my niece and nephew. And the two always had each other growing up. They're practically brother and sister."

"I have a question I'd like to ask you, if you don't mind."

"Sure, Mr. Silver."

"Meeting Agent Brooks in Colorado seems like it was your and Alleen's idea. Why didn't you include Polunu?"

"Ahhh," Malie sighed, "like I said, Polunu can be very hotheaded. At the time, it wasn't a good idea to let him know about it."

"Does it have anything to do with the family feuding?"

Malie didn't answer right away, but after a few moments, said, "Yes, it's because of family issues, and I'll leave it at that."

"Fair enough. Where's Alleen's father?"

Malie again took her time answering. "Let's just say the man who was her father died a long time ago," she finally said. "Oh, look there," she said while pointing at the hut Julia, Alleen, and Polunu had entered with the teenage kid.

Julia and Alleen wore grass skirts with flower tiaras, Polunu was shirtless with briefs and a loincloth, and all three wore leis around their necks. They walked with a few others to the center, near the fire, and stood. The young man handed Polunu a stick with a fireball on each end.

"Does he know how to use that thing?" Silver asked Malie.

"Not to worry; he's one of the best fire twirlers in the village," she said.

"If you say so."

After a minute, the drums, ukuleles, and flutes played, and people danced and cheered. Silver watched as Julia and Alleen waved their arms and swayed their hips from side to side, Polunu yelled some words, then danced around while twirling the stick in his hand. He spun it behind his back, then threw it up in the air and caught it before yelling some more words and dancing. Malie clapped, sang, and bobbed her head the entire performance. In that moment, Silver caught himself smiling and tapping his feet. He even muttered some of the words that Malie was singing. At one point, Silver ogled Julia for a long moment. She noticed and knew he was looking at her and enjoying what he saw. Silver didn't care, because he was captivated.

"You know, she likes you a lot," Malie said.

Silver snapped out of his daze. "Who?"

"Your girlfriend."

"No, we're not together."

"Okay, if you say so," Malie said with a smile.

When the festivities were over, the group went back to Malie's house. Polunu stayed only a few minutes before going to his own home, and Malie retired to her bedroom shortly after, while Silver, Julia, and Alleen all shared her spare room. The room was large, furnished with twin bunk beds and a standalone full-sized bed. Julia and Alleen took the bunk beds, Alleen on the top bunk and Julia on the bottom. Silver, being the largest of the three, took the separate bed. They left the room window cracked open, and a cool draft occasionally swept inside and breezed over Silver. He enjoyed it, thought it felt good. As they lay in the bed, the sounds of the village gradually died down, until only nature's song played through the chirps, hoots, and leaves rustling in the wind.

"I'm truly sorry," Alleen said.

"Don't be," Julia said.

"Yeah, being sorry won't help," Silver said.

"I thought I was doing the right thing. I thought I was helping by getting law enforcement involved. But it looks like I've just made things worse."

"Feeling sorry for yourself won't help either. We've all had a rough day. How about we get some rest and pick this up tomorrow?"

"Lee's right," Julia said, "let's get some sleep."

"Okay, but I want you both to know I truly thank you from the bottom of my heart."

There was a long moment of silence before Julia said, "You're welcome."

"Thank me when it's over," Silver said.

The next morning, Silver woke to sunlight in his eyes and the scent of sausage and egg hitting his nose. Julia and Alleen were still in their beds, moaning and turning in their sleep. Silver rubbed his eyes, yawned, then stretched before finding the bathroom and relieving himself. When he made it back to the room, Julia and Alleen were still in their bunks, but they were talking to one another. Silver didn't interrupt. He just lay on his bed and listened.

"Your auntie sure loves to cook. I don't think I've ever cooked two meals back-to-back," Julia said.

Alleen laughed. "Yes, she does."

"How long do you think it'll take us to make it to your village?"

"Not too long."

"Good, because I want to take it easy today."

"Once we get there you can relax, then we'll work on getting you guys off the island."

"Breakfast's ready," Malie said, standing at the door. "Make your beds, wash up, and come eat."

They did as instructed and went to the table where a plate of eggs, sausage, and rice waited for each of them. Silver was the first to finish his meal. Julia and Alleen took longer, mainly because they were doing a lot of talking. He left them at the dining table and grabbed his wallet and cell phone off the end table in the living room. The wallet he checked then placed in his pocket, and with the cell phone, he connected the battery and pressed the power button. The screen lit up. While the phone booted, he looked at Julia to share the good news with a gesture, but she was still talking. Silver shook his head before turning his attention back to the phone, and to his surprise, it had three bars. The battery was at seventy percent, and there were no missed calls or new emails he cared about. He turned toward the table and saw he had caught Julia's eye.

"It's working," he said with a smile as he waved his phone at her.

"Really!" she said.

"Yep, check yours."

Silver opened the map app on his phone, while Julia finished the few bites remaining on her plate and hustled to her phone. He watched as she inserted the battery and powered it on.

"Looks like it's working," she said.

Silver viewed a map with a blue dot showing his position. He expanded the view and memorized the location before powering off his phone and stuffing it in his pocket.

"Yep, I'm working," Julia continued.

As she uttered those words, Polunu raced into the house, slightly out of breath. "We should get going," he said.

CHAPTER SEVEN

"RIGHT NOW?" ALLEEN asked.

"The moment everyone's ready," Polunu said.

"Come eat breakfast," Malie said to him.

"I've already had breakfast, Auntie," he said before sharing his gaze between Silver and Alleen. "I'll be outside near the hangar. Come as soon as you're ready," he finished before walking out the door.

Alleen scoffed. "Whatever."

"Get ready to go," Silver told Julia before following Polunu. Outside he found dew covered the grass, and from the east, the sun beamed across a partially clouded, orange-tinted sky. The air was cool and filled with the scent of eggs and sausage.

Silver threaded around a few conversing villagers and caught up with Polunu. The two walked together toward the hangar.

"So, what's the big hurry?" Silver asked.

"The sooner I get you guys on the way, the better."

"What's that supposed to mean?"

"It means what I said."

"Why do I get the feeling you're not being straight with me?"

Polunu stopped, and Silver stopped with him.

"I'm not being straight with you?" Polunu said. "Why should I care? I barely know you. But I do know you staying here could cause trouble for the village."

"You mean with Shima and the Yakuza? Are you afraid of him?"

Polunu waved Silver's comment away and continued toward the hangar.

Silver followed behind him. "Is that a yes?" he asked.

"I fear no man, but don't want to cause unnecessary trouble here—for my people," Polunu said as he approached a shed next to the hangar.

A man with an AK-47 stood guard in front.

"What about your cousin? Isn't she your people?" Silver asked.

Polunu snickered. "I'm not worried about them hurting her," he said before turning to the armed guard, nodding, and walking inside.

"What does that mean?" Silver asked Polunu. He then looked at the guard. "I'm with him," he said while pointing at Polunu and following him inside the shed. "Why are you not worried about her? What did you mean?" Silver asked him again.

Polunu walked to a long table covered with rifles, hand-guns, and ammunition. He grabbed a rifle and a magazine. "I mean, I'll be bringing a couple of my men with me to make sure you make it to the village safely."

"You're expecting trouble?"

"It's possible."

"Okay, give me one of those automatic rifles."

Polunu laughed. "Have you ever fired a gun like this?"

"You weren't asking when I had one aimed at you yesterday."

"Pointing a gun at a man and shooting a man are two completely different things. You can hurt yourself or others if you're not careful with these automatics."

"I'll manage," Silver said, as he reached for one of the AK-47s on the table.

"No-no," Polunu said, while blocking Silver's hand. He then picked up a thinner, slightly longer rifle and handed it to Silver. It was an old school lever action rifle with a shoulder strap.

"What's this?" Silver said, holding the gun in his hands.

"It's training wheels."

"Look, this isn't the wild west, we're not robbing a stagecoach."

"Well, that's all we have available. The rest of the guns are for the guards to protect the village. The magazine for it is there," Polunu said, pointing at the table.

Silver flipped the gun, cocked the lever, and inspected the loading port, trigger, and bolt. He then flipped the gun once more and aimed it at the far end of the hangar.

Polunu's eyebrows raised.

"This gun is in great shape," Silver said. "What's the magazine capacity, fifteen?"

"Yeah, I believe so."

"Okay, then," Silver said, grabbing the magazine and draping the rifle over his shoulder.

Silver and Polunu exited the shed and met Julia and Alleen approaching.

"All ready?" Polunu asked.

"No, we just wanted to see you," Alleen said.

"Hey, don't get smart with me. It was your plan that backfired."

"Whatever, can we go?"

Polunu stared at Alleen for a moment before shaking his head and walking to the hangar's side door. He opened it and stuck his head inside. "You guys ready?" he asked. There was a faint response, and Polunu said, "Okay, we'll be out here." He then shut the door and walked back to Silver and the others.

A few moments later, two men carrying AK-47s exited the hangar and approached the group.

"We're ready," one of them said to Polunu.

"Okay, let's go."

The six entered one of the larger jeeps and drove through the grassy field toward the mountain. When the terrain inclined steeply, Polunu instructed his man behind the wheel to stop the jeep and park. The group slid out of the vehicle and hiked up a dirt path. Polunu and one of his armed men lead the way. The other armed guy followed behind Silver, Julia, and Alleen. They snaked up the incline for half a mile before the pathway leveled straight. To their right, the mountainside stood high, overtaken by vines and coated with green vegetation. On the right, a downward slope covered with greenery flowed into a vast body of still turquoise water. Silver saw Julia admiring the view and smiled at her. She smiled back.

The group walked for another mile before reaching a narrow pathway that sloped down into the forest. As they entered the jungle, Silver's phone rang. He reached into his pocket while everyone else continued ahead.

"Silver speaking," he said into the phone while trailing behind the group.

"Oh, there you go. Tried calling you twice; it's Semy."

"Yeah, we were up in the mountains, bad reception, I'm sure."

"How are you guys holding up?"

"We're fine; what do you got?"

"It was hard to find information on Shima, but from what I gathered, he's definitely tied to the Yakuza. He's wanted by multiple law enforcement agencies for kidnapping, drugs, murder, robbery, you name it."

"What else you find?"

"Not much more other than he has properties in Japan and Europe."

"What about Brooks? Did you find anything that ties the two together?" Silver asked as he stepped over a log and fanned a huge leaf from his face.

"No, I didn't see any connection between the two, and from what I can tell Brooks is a boy scout."

"Really?"

"Yep, he's clean from what I saw."

"Of course he is," Silver said with a sigh.

"Oh yeah, I sent you pictures of them, detailing pretty much what I've already told you."

"Thanks, Semy. Can you do me one more favor?"

"Absolutely."

"Do a little more digging to see if Shima has any property in Hawaii."

"Okay, I didn't see anything on my initial search, but I'll give it another pass. He's a hard one to find information on, but I'm going to crack this egg."

"Thank you."

"Be careful."

"I will."

Silver ended the call and opened his phone's email app. He saw an email from Semy and pressed on it. Immediately a picture of Shima displayed with a small paragraph of information below it. Silver thumbed down the email and found a picture of a man with combed-back dirty-blond hair and rigid green eyes. Silver caught up with Alleen and showed her his phone.

"Is this him?" he asked.

Alleen stopped walking, jerked her head back, and squinted. "That's Agent Brooks. Where did you get it?"

Silver pulled the phone away and shook his head. "It came from someone I have looking into him."

"Did they find anything on him?"

"No, says he's clean."

"Doesn't make sense. How else would Shima know I was meeting him?"

"I don't know yet."

Alleen shrugged and followed behind Polunu through the bushes.

Julia approached Silver. "What was that about?" she asked as she wiped the sweat from her forehead.

He turned his phone screen to her. "I had Semy do some digging, just wanted her to confirm this was Brooks."

"So, is it?"

"Yep, and he appears to be squeaky clean."

"Well, let's not trust him yet."

"Believe me, I can't see a reason I should trust him, currently," Silver said, adjusting the lever rifle's straps around his shoulder and continuing through the jungle.

After another twelve minutes of walking, the group came upon a small open garden field. It had collard greens, beans, and fruits similar to the garden in Polunu's village. On the other side of the field were modular homes and huts.

"We made it," Alleen said to Silver and Julia. "It's just past the garden."

When they made it to the garden, the scent of burnt wood drifted in the air. The armed guard who was taking point held up his hand and made a fist. Everyone stopped in their tracks, and Silver spotted a line of smoke rising from the cluster of modular homes and huts. The group quickly took cover behind a large bushel of shrubs.

"They're here," Polunu said.

As he finished speaking, seven loud claps rang from inside the village. Screams and cries soon followed.

"Gunfire," Silver said.

Julia dropped to her knees and covered her head.

"No!" Alleen screamed, racing toward the shots.

Silver grabbed her before she could make it around the shrubs. "Wait, you'll get yourself killed," he said as she fought to break his hold.

Polunu and the two armed men brought their AK-47s to bear and moved in. A moment after they walked around the bushel, five more blasts roared over the sky.

"No! Let me go!" Alleen hollered as Silver wrestled her to the ground next to Julia.

"Stay down," he told them.

Julia threw an arm around Alleen, and the two ducked.

Silver's training kicked in and he scanned the area like he had done many times before. He saw two SUVs and eleven combatants, most armed with Bushmaster XM-15s assault rifles. Shima stood next to the SUV with a smile on his face. On the ground lay the bodies of some villagers, an older man and a teenage girl. They looked maimed, or possibly dead. Before Silver could determine which, one of Polunu's men took a bullet to the arm and cried out in pain. He fell to the ground, but not before shooting one of Shima's men in the gut. Polunu and the other guard dragged their wounded partner to safety and took cover inside a hut. A few of the villagers, armed with AK-47s, returned fire at Shima and his men. It was clear the villagers had no training because they hit nothing.

Shots continued to boom, and people continued to run and scream. Silver looked at Julia. She looked back at him with damp eyes and trembling lips as she continued to cover Alleen. Silver's top priority was to keep Julia safe, and in order for that to happen, he would have to take care of Shima and his men quickly. He removed the lever rifle from over his shoulder and pointed it in front of himself as he stepped from behind the shrubs. His first target was in his sights in a matter of microseconds. He fired a round, cocked the lever, swung his sights to another target, and fired another round, cocked the lever again before finding his third target and firing his third round. Just like that, in one and a half seconds, three of Shima's men were down.

Two more of Shima's cronies opened fire at the hut where Polunu and his men took cover. Silver fired and hit one man in the neck. The other man swung his aim in Silver's direction, but Silver had already fired another round and struck the armed man in the chest. Both men dropped to the ground. Silver raced to them, dropped the lever action rifle, and scooped up one of their assault rifles. He glanced toward the hut and saw Polunu looking at him with wide eyes, and his mouth gaped. Silver smirked, then winked at him before aiming the automatic rifle toward the SUVs, where most of Shima's men retreated. As Silver opened fire, Shima jumped inside the front passenger seat of a vehicle. The bullets thumped and ricochet off the door.

Great bulletproof.

Silver shot two rounds at the window on Shima's side and fractured the glass while three bad guys near the SUV returned fire, forcing Silver to run and dive into a trench. Bullets whizzed and zipped above him as he lay in the damp, cold soil. When the loud blasts paused, and he could no longer hear or feel the bullets crashing into the ground behind him, Silver erected from the trench and let off a few rounds. He hit one of Shima's guys and the man slammed into the SUV before plummeting to the ground. The vehicle then spun off, and Silver jumped from the trench and chased after it. The SUV darted to the center of the village, sending many scurrying out of its path before making a U-turn and cutting through a grass field toward a dirt road. Silver ran after them, but they were moving too fast. When the SUV neared the dirt road, Silver dropped to one knee and aimed the XM-15 at the back window, and unloaded. He held the rifle steady as it kicked against his shoulder and hot, spent shells ejected from the gun. The vehicle's back window shattered, and Silver's rifle clicked empty. The SUV left him watching as it flung a trail of dirt particles in the air behind it.

Loud booms continued to flow from the village. Silver turned and saw a group of villagers firing at the other SUV. The vehicle raced up the dirt road and all the gunfire ceased. Silver dropped the empty rifle and ran back toward the garden. On his way, he saw Polunu helping a local stand up against a tree.

Polunu approached Silver and stared at him for a few seconds. "What is it you said you do for a living?" he finally asked.

Silver smirked and walked over to the lever rifle he dropped earlier, picked it up, and tossed it to Polunu. "Nice training wheels."

Polunu caught the gun and briefly scanned it before shaking his head. "So, where are the girls?"

"They're over here," Silver said while pointing and walking toward the large bushel of shrubs.

Both men looked behind the shrubs, but Julia and Alleen were not there.

"Where are they?" Silver said.

"They couldn't've gone too far."

Silver jogged through the garden with his head on a swivel. "Jules! Jules! Alleen! Where are you guys!" When he didn't find them, he turned to Polunu, who was now on the other side of the garden, and threw his arms in the air. Polunu shrugged, gesturing that he didn't find them either. Silver threw his hands on his hips and, as his head continued to swivel around the field, he noticed a villager approach Polunu.

He jogged over just in time to hear the villager tell Polunu, "Alleen and the other girl were captured."

CHAPTER EIGHT

"NO, NO, NO," Silver muttered before stepping to Polunu. "Where did he take them!"

"I—I don't know," Polunu said.

Silver grabbed him by his collar. "What do you mean you don't know? He has to have a base of operations here."

"He probably does, but that doesn't mean I know where it is," Polunu said as he pushed Silver's hands away. "I'm just as upset as you. These are my people. If I knew, don't you think I would've already hit the place?"

Silver said nothing, just walked away, removed his cell phone, and pressed at the screen before holding it to his ear.

"Semy speaking."

"Semy, Silver, you're gonna have to speed up the search."

"Why, what happened?"

"It's Julia, Shima has her."

"Oh no, I'm looking now."

"Okay, let me know as soon as you find something."

"I will."

Silver ended the call and patted his phone against his

free hand as he gazed at the ground. He remained that way for a minute before walking to Polunu.

"Can you take me back to the resort?" he asked him.

Polunu hunched his shoulders. "Yeah, sure. Just let me patch my man up and we'll be ready to go."

Silver watched as the injured man had his arm wrapped. It was a flesh wound. The bullet entered and exited, but it looked painful.

"How does it feel?" Polunu asked the man.

"I'll live," the man said.

"Good. Let me have a word with them," Polunu said, nodding toward a group of villagers. "We'll leave right after," he concluded as he joined the group of men.

Polunu talked with the villagers for a few minutes before walking back to Silver and his two men. The four men then trekked across the garden and into the jungle. It wasn't long before they exited the forest and traveled uphill into the mountains. The journey back seemed quicker, feeling like it took half the time to reach the jeep than it took to arrive at Alleen's village. The men hopped into the jeep and drove across the grassy field to Polunu's village. At the heart of the village, a crowd welcomed them. Malie stood front and center of the mob.

Silver and Polunu exited the jeep and walked to her.

"What happened? We heard gunfire," she said with a frown. "And where's Alleen? Where's Julia?"

Polunu sighed, looked at the ground, and shook his head.

Malie's eyes narrowed, and her lips trembled. "What— what is it?"

"Shima and his men attacked the village. He captured them." Silver said.

"No," Malie gasped.

Silver put his hand on her shoulder. "Don't worry. I'll get them back."

Polunu turned to his man, the one without the injury. "Gather some fighters and weapons and head to the village in case they return."

The man nodded and raced in the hangar's direction, and as he did, a teenage girl ran to Malie.

"You have a call. It's important, come," she said.

Malie, Silver, and Polunu followed the young lady to Malie's house. When they all entered, the girl snatched the cordless phone from the dinner table and handed it to Malie, who took a moment to catch her breath.

"Hello," she said into the phone.

Malie listened to the caller for a few seconds.

"Yes, you bastard, my number is still the same—"

She listened some more.

"You're not going to hurt her; you better not," Malie said with a crack in her voice.

Silver grabbed the phone and put it on speaker before resting it on the table.

It's him, she motioned with her lips.

Silver nodded.

"You've tried my patience for the last time," Shima said through the phone. "You killed her the moment you two plotted against me. So, when I get the information I need, I'm going to make her disappear, along with this very fine red-bone. But I don't know, I may keep her around for a little while."

Silver's eyebrows dropped, his nose crinkled, his teeth clenched, and his gut bubbled with rage, but he didn't speak.

"Where's fat boy?" Shima asked. "I know he's listening. If you're thinking about coming after me, don't. You may have a big belly, but you're a small fish, and I'll gut you alive."

Polunu frowned, and his eyes narrowed.

Shima chuckled. "What, you have nothing to say? I didn't think so. Where's the army man? I want to talk with him."

"I'm here," Silver said.

"Leroy Silver, is it? You served eight years in the Army with two tours in Afghanistan and have a few commendations. Very impressive resume. Oh, interesting, after your time in the Army, there's ten years unaccounted for. Which means the government had you behind a desk at some top-secret facility, or you were an asset in one of their shadow organizations. Given the show you put on today, my money's on the latter."

Polunu and Malie both looked at Silver with squinted eyes.

"Myself and the Yakuza are willing to forgive you despite the trouble you caused. So, being the businessman I am, I'll make you a deal. I'll give you this red-bone, and you two get off my island and never come back."

"What about, Alleen?" Malie said.

Shima laughed. "She stays with me, where she belongs."

"No!"

"I promise I'm going to—" Polunu started.

"You're going to what?" Shima growled. "You're going to do what I say, or you'll be receiving parts of her for months."

Polunu breathing became heavy, but he said nothing.

"So, Mr. Army, do we have a deal? I'd take it if I was you, especially after what you did to my men yesterday. They're still very upset about it and want some blood."

"Both girls," Silver said. "And we all stay out of your business. That's my counteroffer."

"This is not up for negotiation. Business has been interrupted and someone must pay for it."

"No deal."

"Well, I guess I'll keep them both. What do you say to that, Army?"

"I have nothing else to say to you."

"And why's that?"

"I don't like wasting my breath talking to dead men," Silver said, before ending the call.

"Good call on the deal. He can't be trusted," Polunu said.

Silver nodded. "Yeah, strange he would even offer that."

"It probably was a trap," Malie said. "He would've tried to kill you both."

"Maybe," Silver said before looking at Polunu. "I need to get back to the resort."

"Okay, let's go," Polunu said.

As the two men exited the house, they heard Malie shout.

"Bring her back to us!"

***

Silver sat in the back seat of the jeep next to one of Polunu's soldiers. The afternoon sun beamed, but the wind kept him cool as the jeep hummed along the rough path. Polunu sat in the front passenger seat while another one of his men drove.

"How much further?" Silver asked.

Polunu twisted in his seat to face Silver. "Not long," he said with a headshake. "Are you sure you want to go back? Shima might've placed some of his men there."

"No choice. I have to find the girls."

"How's going back gonna help?"

"Shima's men stayed at the resort, so I'm hoping to find clues on where he could've taken them."

Polunu shrugged. "Okay. I'll let you know when we're close."

"Roger that," Silver said, before removing his phone.

He dialed a number and held it to his ear. It took four rings before there was an answer.

"Anderson speaking."

"Hi Matt, it's Silver."

"Hey, you're a little muffled, are you outside?"

Silver cuffed his free hand over the phone. "Is that better?"

"Yeah, I didn't expect to hear from you so soon. How's the trip?"

"Not good, I had a run-in with the Yakuza."

"What?"

"Yeah, the name Shima ring any bells?"

"Hold on, wait, Kazan Shima?"

"You know him?"

"He's one of the top five on the agency's termination list. We've been looking for him in Asia, but he's in Hawaii?"

"Well, when I get to him, you won't have to worry about it. That bastard has Julia."

"Oh no."

"I'm guessing since you didn't know he was in Hawaii, you don't know where his base could be?"

"No, but I'm looking into it now, and when we find it, I'll have the National Guard storm the place."

"Wait! If you do that, he'll kill the girls. I have to make sure they're out first."

"Girls?"

"Yeah, he doesn't just have Julia. He has someone else. Her name is Alleen."

"Okay…"

"She's a local. It's a long story, but it reminds me, do you have any FBI contacts in Denver?"

"I have FBI contacts across the country."

"Know a Brooks?" Silver asked.

"Jacob Brooks?"

"I guess you do."

"What does he have to do with this?"

"Not exactly sure. Alleen went to Denver to meet him; seems they were working together to put Shima away."

Anderson sighed. "That brings a lot of questions to mind."

"I know, but the short of it is, she had info to incriminate Shima, and her contacts led her to Brooks. She met Brooks in Denver, and he was supposed to have U.S. Marshals escort her to a secure location, but two of Shima's goons showed up at her hotel instead. They brought her back to Hawaii, where Jules and I ran into her."

"Something's off. Shima isn't the type of guy who'll allow someone with incriminating information on him to live."

"Yeah, that's been bugging me too."

"But I understand why her contact would trust Brooks."

"Why's that?"

"He's by the book. I'll be surprised if the guy ever even had a speeding ticket."

"So, no way he could be working with Shima?"

"If you ask me, not a chance. But look, I'm going to find where Shima is, and I'll call you back with what I find."

"Thank you, Matt."

"Anytime. Hey, what are you going to do until then?"

"What I do best."

"I know what that means. Stay by your phone."

"Copy that," Silver said before ending the call.

The jeep bumped onto the highway and merged into traffic. They drove two more miles before pulling off the highway.

Polunu turned to Silver. "We're almost there."

Silver nodded. "I know, the resort's entrance is just up the road."

"Yep, but we don't want to drop you off at the front."

"No, you're right. I want to get in unnoticed," Silver said before hopping out of the jeep and onto the grass.

"We have to get back to the villages. Be careful," Polunu told him.

"I will."

Polunu gave Silver a half-nod before turning to the man behind the wheel and pointing at the road. The jeep pulled off, and Silver watched until it disappeared from sight. He then turned his attention to the seven-foot brick wall that stood in front of the resort and figured it would be best to enter through one of the neighboring properties. He jogged a quarter of a mile before slipping inside the entrance of a neighboring resort. No one said anything or even noticed as Silver strolled up the driveway, into the resort's main lobby, through the back automatic sliding doors, and onto the beach where sand blew in his face, and the scent of salt and sunblock struck his nose. He threaded through a crowd in swimsuits and passed large umbrellas and sandcastles on his way to the water.

The shoreline stretched as far as Silver could see in either direction. He followed it a quarter of a mile toward the targeted resort while the sound of waves crashing, wind gusting, and seabirds squawking intruded his ears. When he made it to the resort, he stood on the beach and scanned the perimeter. No security, nothing suspicious, only vacationers and resort staff entering and leaving the building. Silver blended into the crowd and entered the resort. Inside, two police officers stood in the lobby, one near the front and the other toward the back. The officer at the front watched as two workers replaced the glass for the automatic sliding doors. Silver strolled to the stairwell, unnoticed, and hiked upstairs to his floor. He opened the stairwell door, peeked inside, and made sure the hallway was empty before entering and walking toward the room where Alleen and Shima's men stayed. But as he passed his own room, he noticed something that stopped him in his tracks.

My door is cracked open, he thought to himself as he stepped to the door and slowly nudged it completely open.

Inside, everything looked in order, except for Silver's bed. Some of his clothes, along with his duffel bag, lay on the wrinkled bed comforter. Silver picked up his duffel bag, turned it right side up, and underneath he found his passport, opened. He placed the passport in his pocket, then walked to the adjoining door and peeked into Julia's room. Everything looked in order except her luggage was open with the contents of her purse scattered on her bed. Silver noticed her wallet and license lying on the bed. He tossed everything back into her purse, snatched it off the bed, and walked to the door. When he opened the door, he found a Glock 19M pointed at his face.

CHAPTER NINE

SILVER RAISED HIS hands and back-pedaled into the room. The man followed Silver with the gun still trained on him.

"Who are you, a thief? Trying to steal that purse?" the man asked as the door shut.

"No, this belongs to my friend," Silver said.

"Yeah, right. I'm going to ask again, who are you?"

Silver scanned the man's face and recognized his hair and eyes. "Wait, you're Jacob Brooks, right?"

Brooks squinted his eyes. "Yes, how do you know me?"

"Alleen."

"Alleen? Where is she?"

"Shima has her, and we don't have a lot of time."

"Okay, put your hands behind your back."

"I said we don't have time for that."

"It's procedure. I don't know you."

"Call Matt Anderson, he can vouch for me."

"Wait, you're Leroy Silver?"

"Yes."

"I just talked with Anderson, he told me about you and a

little about what's going on. I'm not working with Shima," Brooks said as he holstered his gun.

Silver lowered his arms and stared at him.

"I wanted to take her to a secure location because my office has ears. When the Marshals got to her hotel, she was gone. I wasn't sure if she got cold feet or what, so I came to Hawaii to track her, and Anderson called me about ten minutes ago—he told me about this resort as I was literally passing by it."

Silver chuckled. "Yeah, he was the one that recommended I stay here. Almost seemed like he planned this."

"Any idea where Shima took Alleen?"

"Not yet. Anderson, of course, is looking into any property Shima owns on the island, and I also have a friend with the NYPD looking into it."

"Okay good. The more hands on deck the better. I have my partner looking into it as well. I guess we have to wait until we hear something."

"Well, I was planning on checking out the room where Shima's men stayed," Silver said as he walked to the door and opened it.

"Do we have a warrant for that?" Brooks asked, walking behind him.

Silver shook his head as he walked up the hall. "You're kidding, right?"

"Well, that would be proper procedure."

Silver turned the doorknob, but the door was locked. "Of course it wouldn't be that easy."

"I have a master keycard; got it from the front desk," Brooks said.

"You have a master keycard, and you're asking about a warrant?"

"Just in case I ran into a situation where I had probable cause."

"Where's the card?"

"Here," Brooks said, removing the card from his pocket.

"Wait, you hear that?" Silver said, placing his ear to the door.

Brooks' eyes widened. "What?"

"Sounds like screams," Silver said before snatching the card from Brooks and buzzing the door open.

"I don't hear anything."

"Oh sorry," Silver said while handing the keycard to Brooks and stepping inside. "My bad, I must've been mistaken."

Brooks shook his head and followed Silver inside.

Silver scanned the room on entry. It looked similar to his, with marble floors, a living area, and a balcony, but there were two queen-size beds instead of one king-size. The beds were made, and the countertops and tabletops were litter-free.

Brooks shrugged. "Well, we're in now. So, anything in particular you hope to find?"

"Anything that can tell us where Shima has taken the girls."

"That'll be challenging. Oahu is a big island. Plus, there are other islands."

"I'm betting he's keeping them on this island or really close by."

"Yeah, some of the other islands have airports so, it would make sense for Shima's men to fly Alleen into the airport closest to their base."

"Exactly. Hey, does this room look a little too neat?" Silver asked as he strolled into the living area.

"Yeah, it's called room service," Brooks said.

Silver saw a wooden vase on an end table. "I don't know," he said, picking up the vase and inspecting it before placing it back on the table. "The door to my room was open. Room service normally does the entire floor unless someone's in the room."

"What are you saying?"

"I think some of Shima's men straightened up in here, enough to make it look like there was never a struggle."

"A struggle?"

"Yeah, Alleen said she hit one of the men with a wooden vase," Silver said, pointing at the vase on the end table. "That vase has a small crack in it."

Brooks walked to the end table and slowly spun the vase. "Yeah, it does," he said. "But that doesn't help us much."

"No, it doesn't."

Brooks walked toward the bathroom, taking a big sniff as he did. "Ah, something smells good."

Silver ignored the comment and walked to the beds, where he found nothing of interest.

Brooks exited the bathroom. "Nothing," he said, shaking his head. He sniffed again. "What's that smell?"

Silver inhaled through his nose. "I know that smell," he said as he looked around the room. He found a trash bin with a plastic cup inside of it. The cup had the words "Keonaona Juice Hut" written on it. "Do you know where this place is?" Silver asked, showing Brooks the cup.

"No, but let me see if I can find it," Brooks said as he removed his phone and typed on the screen. "Says it's in Waialae-Kahala, only fifteen minutes away."

"I knew it. You drove yourself here?"

"Yeah, rented a car."

"Good, let's go," Silver said, while making his way to the door.

"Wait, we're going there based on a cup?"

Silver stopped at the door. "No, based on the owner of the cup."

Brooks nodded. "Right, it probably belonged to Shima or one of his men, but that's still a long shot, don't you think?"

"It beats standing around and waiting. You coming or what?"

They drove six miles in Brooks' rented Ford Explorer before reaching a parking lot near the shore. Next to the lot was a picnic area with a large circular hut toward the back.

Brooks killed the engine and pointed at the hut. "That has to be it," he said.

"It is," Silver said.

"You're pretty sure about it."

"Yep, look how long the line is."

Brooks squinted at Silver.

Silver shrugged. "I've tasted the mangoes from this area, they're incredible."

"Oh."

They stepped out of the Explorer and crossed the lot under the partly cloudy afternoon sky. Silver led the way to the picnic area and past the queue of people. A few customers in the line scoffed and whispered about line cutting as they walked to the hut. Inside, behind the window and counter, stood a short, bulky kid with glasses.

Brooks flashed his badge. "Excuse us," he said to the

patrons standing at the front of the line. We're here on offi-cial law enforcement business."

"Is the owner here?" Silver asked the young man behind the counter.

The kid didn't speak, just nodded, stepped away from the window, and walked toward the back of the hut.

A few moments later, clattering rang from the side of the hut. Silver and Brooks walked around and found a slender man with gray on his face and head exiting the side door.

"Excuse me, sir," Brooks said to him as he flashed his badge. "I'm Jacob Brooks with the FBI. Have a few questions to ask you."

The man's mouth gaped, and his eyebrows rose to his receding hairline.

"Are you the owner here?"

The man nodded and squinted. "Yes, yes sir, I am. Is everything okay?"

"Yes, just have some questions for you."

"Okay, how can I help?"

"Have you noticed anything strange today?"

The man pursed his lips and shook his head. "Nothing I can think of."

"Did you work yesterday?" Brooks asked.

"As a matter of fact, I did."

"Did you notice anything unusual yesterday?"

"Unusual how?"

"An unusual group of people," Silver cut in, "or an unusual vehicle."

"I'm sorry, we're open seven days a week, and I'm here most days, and my memory is not as good as it used to be."

"We understand, sir," Brooks said.

"But you know what," the man said, "the day before yesterday, this main street was cut off for construction. No traffic in or out all day, so I wasn't able to work. I don't know if that helps you any."

The day before yesterday, the same day we arrived in Hawaii, Silver thought.

"Well, we won't take up any more of your time, sir," Brooks said on a sigh, and as he did, the door swung open and a woman with long, curly, dark hair peeked outside.

"We're out of pineapple juice," she said to the owner.

"Okay," he said. "I'll pick some up."

She glanced at Silver and Brooks. "Everything okay?"

"Yes, sweetheart, these gentlemen are with the FBI, investigating unusual activities in the area."

"The FBI, really? Unusual activities? I mean, there was a fight that broke out between two customers earlier, and that SUV with the shattered back window, and then the lady whose dog jumped into the ocean—"

"Wait," Silver said. "There was an SUV?"

"Yes, a couple of hours ago, there were two of them," the lady said before pointing to her right. "They sped past and turned near the old marina."

"Oh, yeah, that's right," the slender man said. "I forgot about that."

Silver pointed in the same direction as the lady. "So, this way to the old marina?" he asked as he back-stepped.

"Yes, it's not too far up the road. You'll see a sign for Old Marina Way. Not sure why they went there; no one ever goes there anymore."

"Thanks," Silver said to her before looking at Brooks and saying, "We have to go."

"Thank you both for your time," Brooks said to the slender man and woman before catching up with Silver, who was nearly in the parking lot.

The two entered the Explorer.

"Want to share what you found out?" Brooks asked Silver.

"Earlier today, I shot out the back window of Shima's SUV, and there were two SUVs. One had Julia and Alleen in it."

"That's good enough for me," Brooks said as he fired up the engine.

They veered out of the parking lot and snaked a quarter of a mile up the road before reaching the turn for Old Marina Way. Brooks took a right onto the street, and they drove another fifty yards before Silver held up his hand.

Brooks hit the brakes. "What is it?" he asked.

"See that?" Silver said, pointing one hundred yards up the road at a chain-link fence.

Brooks squinted at the windshield. "Yeah, it's a gate. Looks like it's wide enough for the car to get through."

"I think we should peek around before driving straight in there."

"Yeah, you're right," Brooks said as he reached behind his seat into a bag and removed a pair of binoculars. He then eased the Explorer off the road, and they exited the car. They crept across the grass and up a mound.

"Keep your head down," Silver told Brooks as the two ducked behind a bush.

Brooks peeked over the bush with his binoculars. "Excellent. We can see the entire marina from here, and you're right; I see at least two armed men."

"Let me see," Silver said, grabbing the binoculars. He scanned the area and noticed the fence encompassed the front portion of the marina. A plot of land ran beyond the fence line and into a wooden dock surrounded by old, dented and rusted boats. Two men stood on the dock, one near the gate entrance and the other near the west corner, both with Uzis strapped over their shoulders. At the east corner stood a large, open boat shed. Silver saw movement inside, and seconds later, the clean shaved man who was with Alleen earlier stepped out. He didn't have an Uzi, just a cigarette in his mouth and a lighter in his hand.

Silver removed the binoculars from his eyes and sighed.

"What is it?" Brooks asked.

"There's three men."

"Oh, I guess I missed one."

"The guy with the tapered haircut near the boat shed," Silver said, handing the binoculars to Brooks.

The FBI agent held the binoculars to his face and looked in that direction.

Silver adjusted himself and glanced at the Explorer, then behind himself. "He's one of the men I saw with Alleen," he said to Brooks before turning back and surveying the fence line.

Brooks lowered the binoculars. "I'm going to call to see if I can expedite a warrant," he said as he dug into his pocket.

"A warrant? Really? There's no time for that."

"What do you suggest?"

"I have an idea, but you may not like it," Silver said with a smile.

CHAPTER TEN

FOUR MINUTES LATER, Silver watched as Brooks skulked down the hill. He waited until the FBI agent entered the Explorer before lurking down the opposite side of the hill, toward the west corner of the marina. He took cover near a tree, behind some tall, dense underbrush. Ten yards in front of him was the fence, and on the other side of it, the man with the Uzi stood on the dock next to a dismantled boat. Silver glanced toward the front of the marina and saw the other armed man pacing back and forth. The third man, the one with the clean shave and tapered haircut, was inside the boat shed, out of Silver's line of sight.

"Okay Brooks, it's on you," he said to himself. A couple seconds later, the horn from the Explorer blared across the marina.

The armed man near the front quickly pivoted toward the gate with his Uzi aimed in that direction. The man closest to Silver looked toward the front gate. While the two men fixed on the Explorer, Silver raced from behind the underbrush and sprinted to the fence. He cleared the fence, dashed to the dock, and took cover behind the dismantled boat. As the horn blasted again, the man with the tapered cut jogged from the boat shed and joined his partner at the gate. The guy near Silver walked in that direction, but Silver grabbed him in a rear chokehold, and pulled him behind the boat. The man squirmed and flapped his arms while gasping for air. Silver dropped to his knees, and his opponent went to sleep. He then took the Uzi off the man's body and darted toward the front gate where the clean shaved man and the other guy with the Uzi were barking orders over the roaring horn. The honking stopped as Silver approached the men from behind, with the Uzi trained on them.

"Hands up!" he said.

Both men raised their hands, and Brooks exited the Explorer.

"Turn around, carefully," Silver told the two men with their hands raised.

They both slowly faced him.

The clean shaved man winced when he saw Silver's face. "You," he said.

"Yeah me. How's your jaw? It looks a little swollen," Silver said.

"I'll pay you back for it."

"The only thing you're gonna do is tell me where the girls are."

The man smirked. "Oh, your little girlfriends? Who knows? They could be in the ocean by now."

Silver felt heat rush through his body. His nostrils flared, and his eyebrows arched down. "Last chance."

The man grinned and chuckled.

Silver fixed on him with a hard stare.

The guy with the Uzi draped over his shoulder lowered his arms and reached for the gun.

Without looking at him, Silver shot him twice, center mass. The man flopped backward and plopped onto the deck.

The clean shaved man jerked back and gasped.

"Silver! What are you doing?" Brooks yelled from the opposite side of the gate.

Silver pointed the gun back at the man with the tapered hair.

"Okay, okay, I'll take you there," the man said.

"That's more like it," Silver said. "Now, be a good boy and open the gate for my friend."

The man walked toward the gate and unlocked it.

Brooks pushed the gate opened and ran to the man sprawled on the deck. "What happened? I thought no one would get hurt in your plan," he said, kneeling and placing his hand on the man's neck.

"Well, sometimes things don't go according to plan," Silver said.

"This man is dead."

"I'm touched. I just saw these murders mow down a village full of innocent women and children."

Brooks shook his head.

"Now, take me to them," Silver told the clean shaved man.

The man pointed at the boat shed. "We'll have to take the boat," he said. "They're on an island about two miles offshore."

Silver walked the man to the boat shed at gunpoint while Brooks went back to the Explorer. Inside the shed were two berths. One was empty, and the other had a tarp-covered boat parked at it. The man with the tapered cut removed the tarp, exposing a speedboat.

Brooks entered the boat shed with binoculars in hand.

"Looks like there's a small island a little ways offshore," he said to Silver.

Silver grabbed the binoculars. "Keep an eye on him," he told Brooks.

Brooks removed his Glock 19M and pointed at the clean shaved guy while Silver exited the boat shed, walked to the edge of the dock, and peered through the binoculars. In the middle of the water sat the silhouette of a hilly strip of land.

Silver went back inside the boat shed. "Okay, let's go," he said, handing the binoculars back to Brooks.

"I have to call this in first," Brooks said.

"No, not yet. We need to check out the island first. I don't want to take any chances."

"Well, I can't just leave an active crime scene."

Silver shook his head. "Things are not always black and white, Brooks."

"They could be."

"I don't know about that."

"Why?"

"Because men like me were created to operate in the gray, or whatever color we have to."

Brooks' mouth open but he said nothing.

"When we get eyes on the island, then call in what happened here at the dock," Silver said.

Brooks nodded and two minutes later, the three men were in the speedboat, bumping over the waves. The guy with the taper drove while Silver and Brooks sat in the seats behind him. The droning from the boat's engine and the hissing wind made it difficult to hear. Silver's phone vibrated, and when he checked the caller id, he saw it was Semy. He declined the call and texted her.

You find something?

She replied with, *Yes, we need to talk.*

Small island a couple miles off the coast of Waialae-Kahala?

Yes???

Figured it out. OMW there now.

How?

Boat.

Ok. Call when you can.

Ok.

Silver placed his phone in his pocket.

"Who was that?" Brooks asked.

"A friend."

"What?" Brooks held his hand over his ear.

"My friend with the NYPD," Silver said, louder. "The one I was telling you about earlier. She called to tell me about the island."

Brooks nodded.

Three minutes later, the boat slowed, and the engine revved down to a purr. The island's coast came into view, with white sand and palm trees occupying the shoreline. The clean shaved man veered the boat to the south side of the island.

Silver pointed his gun at the man. "Where are you going?"

The guy glanced over his shoulder. "Toward the mountains. Coming in directly on the shore wouldn't be a good idea."

"This better not be a trick."

"A trick? When he finds out I'm responsible for bringing you here, I'm as good as dead. No trick, I just want to survive."

"He's right," Brooks said to Silver. "If we came in on the shore, we'd be wide open, and I'm sure that's where they'd expect someone to come."

Silver lowered his gun. "I guess so. This is a small

island," he said. "What'd you say, about half a mile from one end to the other?"

Brooks shrugged, "If that. Well, now that we've seen the island, I'm calling in the incident at the marina."

"Can you wait until I get eyes on the girls first?"

"Right now, my cell phone signal is good. I'm not sure how good it'll be on the island."

The guy with the tapered cut looked over his shoulder. "This area has good cell reception. There are cell towers on all the islands in the area, including this one."

"There you have it," Silver said to Brooks.

Brooks sighed. "Okay, but the moment we get eyes on them, I'm calling in everything."

Silver nodded. "Deal."

The boat bounced over the waves for a few more minutes before cruising to the stony side of the island's shore. Brooks exited the boat first, followed by the clean shaved man, and Silver climbed out last with the boat anchor in hand. He stepped onto the rocks before searching the ground and wedging the anchor between two large stones.

"How do we get to them?" Silver asked the clean shaved guy.

The man pointed toward the mountain. "Just on the other side."

"Okay, let's go," Sliver said while aiming his Uzi at the man. "You're our tour guide."

The group walked inland, and Silver's phone vibrated in his pocket, but he ignored it as they continued to the jungle line.

The man led them through the jungle and up a rocky incline. Five minutes later, they crouched on a hilltop, looking down at a mansion.

Brooks scanned over the area through his binoculars. "I see armed men. I'm calling this in," he said.

Silver's phone again vibrated. "Hold on," he said to Brooks before answering the phone. "Silver here."

"It's Anderson. I have some information for you—"

"White mansion on a small island about two miles off the coast of Waialae-Kahala?"

"Yeah—"

"You guys are getting slow at the agency. Semy beat you, and I beat her."

"I take it you're there?"

"Yeah, with Brooks. We've got eyes on the mansion."

"Oh, Brooks is with you? Have you located Julia and your other friend?"

"Not yet."

"Look, I can have the National Guard there within minutes."

"I have to find the girls first, and that may not be necessary."

"I can't let Shima get away, so what do you want me to do?"

"Have the troops on standby while I do some reconnaissance. If you don't hear from me, or you feel something is off, then do what you have to do."

"Roger that."

"Over and out," Silver said, as he ended the call. "What are you seeing?" He asked Brooks.

"I'm calling this in," Brooks said, reaching into his pocket.

"Wait, we have to make sure the girls—"

"I see Alleen down there with another woman."

"What? Why didn't you—let me see," Silver said with his hand out.

Brooks gave him the binoculars.

Silver looked and saw a circular guard shack. Through the shed's windows, he noticed two guards inside. He swung his sights closer to the mansion and saw two more sentries, each standing at opposite corners in front of the house. Just as Silver swung his sights to track the women, he heard ruffling, followed by a thump. When he removed the binoculars from his eyes, he saw the clean shaved guy running down the incline back toward the shore.

Both Silver and Brooks aimed their guns at him. "Hold your fire; they'll hear us," Silver said.

"He's getting away," Brooks said.

"We'll have to deal with him later. Do you still see the girls?"

"Yeah, over there," Brooks said with his finger pointed.

With the binoculars, Silver followed the FBI agent's finger and saw both Julia and Alleen being escorted by an armed guard toward a compact unit that sat separate and apart from the main house.

Brooks raised his phone to his ear. "Yes, this is agent Jacob Brooks..." is all Silver heard as Brooks stepped away and out of earshot.

Silver watched until Julia, Alleen, and the guard disappeared inside the small house. He then looked at the front door of the mansion and saw Shima exiting the house, along with a tall man in khakis and a polo shirt. The man had an athletic build, tan skin, and a crew cut.

Brooks walked back over. "I just called it in. Local law enforcement should be here soon."

"Well, I better hurry then," Silver said, still looking at the Shima and the tall man. "No telling who Shima has on his payroll in the local PD."

"No, this is a local FBI unit, don't worry," Brooks said as

he tapped at his phone. "I'm going to call my partner and fill him in," he said while placing the phone to his ear.

Silver watched as Shima and the man in the polo shirt smiled and conversed. Brooks' phone rang once, then twice, and on the third ring Silver noticed the man talking to Shima remove his cell phone from his pocket. He looked at the phone, then put it back in his pocket and continued chatting with Shima.

"Hey Brooks," Silver said, still looking through the binoculars.

"Hold on, Silver, I'm making a call," Brooks told him. "Pick up, pick up."

"That's what we need to talk about."

Brooks removed his phone from his ear. "He's not answering. What is it?"

Silver looked at Brooks. "Is your partner a young, tall, tan guy, normally sports a crew cut?"

Brooks squinted. "Yeah, why?"

"I think I know why he's not answering your call," Silver said, handing Brooks the binoculars and nodding toward the mansion.

Brooks stared at Silver for a moment before looking into the binoculars. He watched for a few seconds and his lips quivered. "That sleazy bastard," he said on a gasp.

CHAPTER ELEVEN

"WELL, AT LEAST we know how they found out where Alleen was in Colorado," Silver said.

Brooks lowered the binoculars. "Huh? What?" he said.

"When Alleen saw you in Colorado, did you tell your partner?"

"Yeah, but I didn't tell him where she was staying, so I didn't think he had anything to do with it."

"He could've followed her."

Brooks sighed and shook his head. "Miller, you scumbag, I'm going to bust you."

Silver grabbed the binoculars from him and watched as Shima and Miller shook hands before swinging his sights to the small house where Julia and Alleen were.

"Okay, I'm going down to that guest-house. It's like right below us, so should be quick and easy," he said to Brooks.

Brooks said nothing.

Silver looked at him. "Did you hear me?"

Brooks was glaring at the mansion. "Yeah-yeah, you want to go after the girls. But there's a tall fence you'll have to get around."

Silver raised the binoculars and peered down at the guest-house. "I see a tree I can climb to get over the fence. Okay," Silver said, before viewing the front of the mansion once more. He saw Shima had walked back inside the house while Miller made his way across the yard and toward the guard shack. "Looks like Miller is leaving."

"Really? Hand me the field glasses."

Silver did as he asked, and Brooks watched as Miller walked toward the front entrance.

Silver stared at the guest house. "Be on the lookout, I'm heading down there," he said. When he didn't get an answer, he glanced in Brook's direction and saw him duck-walking down the hill toward the front of the property.

"Brooks!" Silver called to him in a loud whisper.

The FBI agent didn't stop or even look back, just continued until he disappeared from Silver's line of sight.

"Great," Silver growled to himself before lurking down-hill toward the guest-house. When he arrived at the tree near the small house, he climbed it until he cleared the top of the fence. He then crawled across a branch into the property before hanging from the branch and dropping to the ground. A bird chirped and flew from the tree, and when Silver glanced at the bird flying across the sky, he saw a security camera hanging from the soffit of the guest house's roof, pointed at him.

Silver dashed to the small house and placed his back against the wall, out of the camera's field of view. "They didn't see me; they didn't see me," he whispered to himself. He stayed that way for a few moments, hoping what he told himself was true. He looked to the front of the guest-house, figuring he could inch along the wall and stay clear of the camera's view, maybe. Before he could take the first step, his phone vibrated once. He looked at the screen and saw a text from Semy.

You should call me now!

Silver ignored the message, placed the phone back in his pocket, and eyed the camera to make sure he wasn't in the frame. His phone vibrated once more, then again, and a third time before he answered it.

"I can't talk right now, Semy."

"Trust me, we should talk, Leroy."

"Why?"

"Because I just saw you on camera."

"Wait—what? How? Oh, did you hack Shima's system?"

"Yep. I can see the live feed, but I have them monitoring on a loop."

"You know I love you, right?"

"Hey, hey, enough of the mushy stuff."

"Is there a camera inside the guest-house?"

"Yeah, I can see Julia and the other woman inside, no guards or anything. I should be able to get you inside."

"That'd be great."

"The door has a digital and manual lock combo. I can hack the digital piece to get you inside."

"Got it, let me get to the front door," Silver said while aiming the Uzi in that direction with his free hand. He paused and flattened his back to the wall when he saw a guard jogging from the mansion toward the guest-house. "Someone's coming," he said to Semy. After a few seconds, he heard the guest house's door beep open, then shut close. "Sounds like they went inside."

"Yep, I see a guard walking into the room with the girls," Semy said.

"Okay, what else?"

A few seconds passed before Semy said, "Looks like he's taking the other girl with him."

"Alleen."

"Yeah, he's taking her."

Silver heard the door buzz open. He peeked and saw the guard walking Alleen toward the mansion. "I see them," he told Semy.

When Alleen and the guard entered the mansion, Silver darted to the guest house's front door, keeping low to avoid detection. "I'm at the door," he said to Semy.

"Okay," she said, and a moment later, the door beeped open.

"Thanks Semy, I'm signing off now."

"Okay, I unlocked Julia's room door. I'll keep an eye out, be safe."

"I will, over and out." Silver ended the call and eased inside the guest-house. He entered a foyer that flowed into a fully furnished living room and a kitchen. Footsteps thumped from a hall on the opposite side of the room. When Silver peeked down the hall, he saw Julia walking in his direction. He threaded through the living quarters and into the hall before embracing her.

"Are you okay? Did they hurt you?" he asked.

She squeezed him. "No, I'm fine," she said.

They released their embrace, and Julia gasped.

"They have Alleen," she said.

"I know, I'll go after her, but I'm getting you out of here first." Silver turned and walked toward the living room with his Uzi aimed in front of him. A tube-shaped camera hanging from the hallway's ceiling caught his eye. He stopped and raised his thumb to the camera.

Julia grabbed his shoulder. "What are you doing? That's a camera," she said.

Silver shook his head, "Don't worry, Semy hacked their system and put them on a continuous loop."

"Oh."

Silver walked into the kitchen and rummaged through the cabinets and drawers.

"What are you looking for?"

Silver found a pair of wire cutters. "This'll work," he said, placing the cutters in his pocket and walking to the front door. "Stay close to me," he told Julia before cracking the door open and peeking outside. "And stay low," he further instructed

They exited the guest-house and crept to the fence line, near the tree Silver had climbed earlier. He knelt, removed the cutters, and snipped the links until a slit formed in the fence.

"That should be enough for you to get through," Silver said as he peeled the split apart.

Julia crawled through the opening to the opposite side of the fence.

Silver handed her the Uzi. "Here," he said while pointing behind her. "I want you to go uphill and lie low. If I'm not back in ten minutes, head to the shore and find a good place to hide until the authorities come."

"What I'm I supposed to do with this?" Julia said, raising the Uzi with both hands.

"Shoot anyone who comes after you, anyone. Oh wait, try not to shoot Brooks."

"The FBI guy? He's here?"

"Yeah, somewhere. Now go."

"Lee, be careful."

Silver winked at her, then watched as she made her way uphill and out of sight. He remained low and followed the fence line toward the back of the mansion, where he saw a side door and an armed guard strolling up and down the sidewall. Silver ran from the fence line and took cover behind grass hedges near a palm tree. He waited until the guard walked toward the back of the mansion before bolting to the armed man and grabbing him in a chokehold. The man swung his arms and bucked, but after eight seconds, he fell asleep. Silver took the man's Uzi and strapped it over his own shoulder. In the guards' pocket was a keycard, so Silver took that too and dragged the man's body to the door before swiping at the door's keycard reader and pulling the man inside the mansion.

The room had a couple of large commercial washing machines and dryers and a few tables. One washer hummed, and piles of clothes lay on the floor and tabletops. Silver dragged the man's body to a walk-in closet. The fumes of linen and washing detergent struck his nose as he sat the man against the closet's back corner wall. Silver left the closet and walked toward a door with an overhead camera aimed at him. He waved at the camera and smiled, knowing Semy had her eyes on him. The door had a circular glass window, which Silver used to look into the adjacent room. He saw two treadmills, a weight machine, dumbbells, and wall mirrors, but didn't see any people. With the Uzi trained in front of him, Silver entered the gym, where he immediately heard a noise coming from another door, which also had a circular glass window.

Silver looked through the window, through a cloud of smoke, and saw two men at a pool table talking. Both men had cigars in their mouths, and both had pool sticks in hand. One wore a cap and stood laughing, while the other, dressed in green camo pants, arched over the pool table and struck the cue ball with the pool stick. In the back corner, three Uzis rested against the wall, and on the opposite wall sat a couch. Silver entered the room with his gun aimed at the man with the cap. The man raised his arms with the pool stick in one hand. The other guy stood up from the pool table and did the same.

"The girl, where is she?" Silver asked.

The men said nothing, but both their eyes flicked to Silver's right side.

In that moment, Silver realized something. *There are three guns in the corner, so three guys.*

The third guy charged from the right, slapping Silver's gun out of his hands and lifting him in a bear hug. Silver felt the man's firm biceps flex around him as he twisted from side to side to break free. The other two men rushed in, but Silver raised his legs and planted his heels in the face of one and into the chest of the other. The one in the camo pants dropped to his knees with his hand to his face, while his partner in the hat stumbled back but quickly found his footing. He axed his pool stick at Silver, but Silver weaved out of the stick's path, and it struck the head of the muscular man that held him. The man released Silver and his hands immediately went to the top of his own head.

The guy in the hat took another swing at Silver.

Silver grabbed the stick and yanked it, along with his attacker, until the man in the hat smacked into the pool table and doubled over it. The pool stick rolled onto the table, and the balls on the table dispersed as Silver snatched two of them, one in each hand, and clapped them simultaneously on both sides of the man's head. The guy's hat fell from his head as he collapsed to the floor.

The man in the camo pants stood, wiping his bloody nose and glaring at Silver. The muscular man growled and glared at Silver as well. Silver snatched the pool stick from the table and broke it in half over his knee. The guy in the camo threw a punch, but Silver hit his arm with one piece of the stick, then his jaw with the other stick, knocking the man into the pool table.

A grunt flowed from behind Silver. He turned to find the muscle man blitzing at him with a haymaker. Silver ducked before striking the man in the knee with a stick, then in his groin with the other stick. The big man bent over and growled as Silver concluded his assault by smacking the man's face with both sticks simultaneously. The muscular man's head rocked back, and he plunged backward until his body hit the floor. Silver tossed the pool stick pieces on the table and turned to find the guy in the camo pants wobbling toward the Uzis. Silver snagged the cue ball from the table and threw it at the man. The ball connected with the back of the man's head and the force knocked him face-first into the wall, then back first to the floor.

Silver slapped the man in the face to keep him conscious. "The girl?"

"Why would I tell you?" the man said.

Silver grabbed his nose and twisted it.

The man hollered. "S—she's upstairs in the study," he said.

"Thank you," Silver said, before punching the man and knocking him unconscious.

He then picked up his own gun and zipped to the door on the opposite side from the one he had entered. The door didn't have a window, so Silver cracked it a slit and heard talking. He promptly closed the door and could no longer hear talking. Silver inspected the door frame and noticed the wall was nearly eight inches thick. *Sound proof?* he thought with a shrug. He ejected the magazine clips from the three Uzis in the corner, tossing all three of the guns in a trash bin and two of the three magazines he slid under the couch. The third magazine, he tucked in the back of his pants. Cracking the door open once more, he heard nothing, so he peeped through the slit and saw a large, empty foyer with a grand staircase. It didn't take him long to dash across the foyer and upstairs.

Ebony-colored hardwood flooring ran throughout the entire second floor. It was quiet, almost too quiet, Silver thought, before seeing a slender guard walk down the hallway to a set of double doors at the end of the hall. Silver took cover behind the corner near the hallway's entrance. A moment later, three knocks flowed through the hall. Shortly after, a door handle jangled, and the door's hinges creaked.

"What is it? Aren't you supposed to be downstairs?" a muffled voice said.

That sounds like Shima, Silver thought.

"Sorry to bother you, sir," a second voice said. The guard, Silver figured. "Takata is watching downstairs. I wanted to let you know I'll be here on the second floor if you need anything."

"Whatever, just make sure I'm not disturbed," Shima said before the door slammed shut.

The guard scoffed. "Jerk."

Silver heard his footsteps approaching, and just when the guard reached the corner, Silver trained the Uzi on him.

The slender man stopped in his tracks, and Silver gestured for him to remain silent, but the man attempted to lift his own gun.

Silver kicked him in the groin, then slapped him with the butt of the gun. As the guard toppled over, Silver caught him and gently settled him on the floor. Silver opened the first door to his right in the hall. The room had four couches and a big-screen TV. Silver dragged the guard inside the room and laid him on the floor before exiting the room and walking to the double doors at the end of the hall. He knocked three times and took a quick glance over his shoulder as he waited.

The door opened. "I thought I told you—" Shima said as his eyes widened when he saw Silver. "Army man."

"In the room," Silver said, with the gun to Shima's face.

Shima stepped backward and Silver entered, shoving him further inside before closing and locking the door behind himself.

"Where's Alleen?" Silver said, scanning the room. He saw a sofa, bookshelves, and a desk before noticing Alleen looking at him from over the back of a Victorian style chair.

She stood. "Silver," she said, dashing to him in handcuffs.

"Where's the key?" Silver asked Shima.

Alleen walked to Shima and fished her hand in his front pocket. "I saw him put it in his pocket," she said before removing her hand and producing a key.

"You're able to unlock it?"

"Yeah—you came for me."

"Of course," Silver said to her before turning to Shima. "Okay, I usually don't do this, but I'm feeling generous. Where do you want it? Head, chest, gut, you tell me."

Shima's mouth fell open and his breathing became heavy. "What reason do you have to kill me?"

Silver tilted his head, and wrinkles crossed his forehead. "Hmm, let me see... you kidnapped my friends, murdered innocent people right in front of me, ruined my vacation, you're involved in organized crime, and did I mention—I just don't like you."

"I'm not a perfect man," Shima said.

Silver nodded. "You think?"

"But is there a crime in wanting to speak with my family?"

"Your family? What are you talking about?"

"Oh, she didn't tell you," Shima said, pointing at Alleen.

Silver glanced at Alleen. "Tell me what?" he asked her.

Alleen looked away.

"Alleen is my daughter," Shima said with a smirk.

CHAPTER TWELVE

"IS WHAT HE'S saying true?" Silver asked.

"Yes, unfortunately," Alleen said.

"Why didn't you say anything?"

"Too embarrassed, I guess. I'm the daughter of a man who murdered his own wife."

"I never meant for anything to happen to your mother!" Shima said.

"But yet she's dead, along with Polunu's parents."

"I didn't pull the trigger; I wasn't even at the village that day."

"But the men who did were after you because of your involvement with the Yakuza."

"I took care of the situation."

Alleen scoffed. "What? By killing them? Mom was already dead."

"Everything I did, I did for you and your mother. Including getting involved with the Yakuza."

Alleen shook her head and tears ran down her cheeks, but she said nothing.

"Enough," Silver said. "I'll ask you again before I decide for you—head, chest, or gut?"

"You don't want to do that, Army," Shima said. "I have strong ties with one of the most notorious organized crime syndicates. They'll hunt you down."

"He's lying," Alleen said. "When the guard was bringing me upstairs, I overheard two other guards." She looked at Shima. "They mentioned you're no longer involved with the Yakuza, and they're actually looking for you."

Shima's eyes dropped to the floor.

With his gun still aimed at Shima, Silver chuckled. "Doesn't sound like things are going your way. Your daughter's turning you into the authorities, and the organization you ruined your family for is after you." Silver lowered his gun. "No, I'm not going to kill you, not yet at least." He turned to Alleen, "Cuff his hands in front of him."

Alleen put the handcuffs on Shima.

"You're going to do this to your own father?" Shima said.

"Man, be quiet," Silver said as he walked behind Shima and pushed him toward the door, "Let's go."

Silver, Alleen, and Shima all trekked downstairs, then into the game room, through the gym, past the laundry room, and outside the house. The sun had begun its descent as an early evening breeze swept through the island. Silver checked the yard and didn't see any guards on the intended path.

"Let's go," he said, pushing Shima along with Alleen following.

They went to the area of the fence where Julia had crawled through earlier.

"You go first," Silver said to Alleen. When she made it to the other side, Silver pointed the Uzi at Shima. "Your turn."

Just as Silver finished uttering those words, he saw

Alleen's eyes widen and her mouth part. He glanced over his shoulder, and behind him, a guard approached. The guard stopped when he saw them. He looked at Shima, then Silver, and then Shima again.

"What are you waiting for you idiot? Shoot him!" Shima said.

The guard raised his gun and fired a few rounds.

Silver dropped to the ground and heard bullets whizzing over his head as he fell out of the line of fire. Before landing belly first on the lawn, Silver shot two rounds. One missed the guard completely, but the other caught him in his shoulder. The man spun and dropped his weapon on his descent to the ground. Silver surveyed the situation. Alleen lay ducked on the other side of the fence, the two guards near the front of the house dashed toward him, and Shima ran toward the circular guard shack.

Silver crawled to a squat. "Head to the top of the hill! Find Julia!" he said to Alleen.

She started up the hill while he sprinted after Shima, who lost balance and stumbled to his knees. Silver grabbed him by the back of his shirt, yanked him up, and pushed him along toward the front gate. The two men in the guard shack exited and joined chase with the other two guards. Silver saw the group of men quickly gaining ground, so he aimed his Uzi at them and opened fire. Seven hot shells, along with seven ear ringing blasts were discharged from the gun. One man took a bullet to the leg, and the other three scattered while returning fire.

Silver grabbed Shima and ducked behind a colossal marble statue of a lion near the front gate. Bullets zipped past, and chips of marble flung through the air.

"Don't shoot me, you morons!" Shima shouted.

The gunfire ceased and Silver stood, holding Shima in

front of himself with his gun aimed at the back of his head. "Come any closer and I'll shoot him!"

As Silver took a step back toward the gate, the men stepped closer with their guns trained on him. Silver stopped and pushed his gun's muzzle into the back of Shima's head. "You think I won't kill him?"

"Stand down—stand down! Lower your guns," Shima told the men.

They did as instructed, and Silver continued to walk backward toward the gate. He kept the gun on Shima before opening the gate and walking through. He pulled Shima along and had him close the gate when they were on the other side.

Shima's men didn't move, just watched while Silver held the gun to their boss and made his way toward the woods.

Silver glanced to his left, uphill, hoping he would see Alleen and Julia, but he didn't, so he continued back-stepping toward the jungle. When the hill blocked his view of Shima's men, Silver yanked his prisoner and dashed through the jungle.

"You know my men are going to kill you," Shima said between pants.

Silver said nothing, just glanced over his shoulder and pushed Shima along. They ran for three minutes before the coastline came into view. The sound of rocks shuffling came from the right, and when Silver aimed his gun in the direction, he saw Alleen coming down an incline. She met them at the edge of the jungle.

Silver looked behind her before hunching his shoulders, "Where's Julia?" he asked.

"She wasn't there," Alleen said.

"What do you mean she wasn't there?"

Alleen hunched her shoulders, "I—I don't know she wasn't there."

Shima chuckled, "Maybe she's dead," he said.

Silver struck the side of Shima's head with the butt of the Uzi, "Shut up!" he told him.

Voices, along with bushes and leaves ruffling, flowed from the jungle.

"I have to go back for her, but you need to get out of here. We used a boat; it's over there," Silver said to Alleen as he pointed in the direction.

The three dashed there, but the speedboat was gone.

"Great, he must've taken it," Silver said.

Shima laughed.

"Who?" Alleen asked.

"It doesn't matter," Silver said, with his head on a swivel. "Up there." He pointed at a cliff. "We need to get to higher ground."

As they ran up the incline, Silver glanced over his shoulder and saw Shima's men exit the jungle and race in their direction. On top of the cliff sat two large stones. Silver and Shima ducked behind one while Alleen took cover behind the stone across from them.

"What now?" she asked.

"We have to shoot our way out," Silver said.

"They're going to kill you," Shima said before chuckling.

"You better hope not, because if I at all feel one of us is going to die, I'll shoot you in the head before that happens."

Shima's chuckle stopped, and his lips flattened.

They sat in silence for a moment. The only sounds came from the birds squawking and the waves crashing twenty-five feet below them near the bottom of the cliff.

"Hand him over!" a deep voice said.

Silver peeked around the stone and saw four armed

guards and the burly guy he fought in the poolroom. The big guy had a black eye and swollen jaw. *I thought for sure he'd still be out*, Silver thought.

"I won't ask again!" the muscle man said.

Silver stood with Shima in front of him and his gun to his head. "I'll shoot him! Get back!"

One guard shot a round. The bullet grazed the large stone and ricocheted toward the ocean.

Silver quickly took cover behind the stone, dragging Shima down with him.

"You idiot! You almost hit me!" Shima yelled at the guard.

Silver looked at Alleen. "Stay low," he told her before bringing his Uzi to bear over the stone and emptying his magazine at the group of men. He hit two of them and they fell to the ground while the other two and the big guy scattered and returned fire. Silver sunk to his knees as the bullets struck the stone and whizzed overhead.

"Two down," he said to Shima as he reloaded the Uzi with the spare mag in his waistband.

"Silver..." a faint voice called.

He looked at Alleen, thinking her voice was faint because of the ringing from the machine gun blasts, but she sat crouched with her head down and mouth close.

"Hey Silver..." the voice said again, this time a little louder.

Silver looked over the cliff and saw a small yacht floating below. He smiled when he noticed Julia on the deck waving at him. "Our ride's here, Alleen," he said. "I'm going to provide cover fire. When I do, I want you to run and jump into the water, understand?"

She nodded.

"That's my boat," Shima said.

Silver ignored him and looked at Alleen. "Okay, let's go," he said, standing from behind the stone with Shima in hand and unloading the Uzi.

The two remaining guards and the big guy flattened to the ground, using the elevated terrain as cover. Alleen sprinted to the edge and jumped off the cliff. Silver kept shooting until the Uzi clicked empty. Throwing his gun down, he dashed to the edge and jumped while pulling Shima with him. Alleen splashed into the water first, then Silver splashed, and while underwater, he heard another immediate splash. He grabbed Shima and heard what could have been yet another splash as they swam to the surface. *Probably just the waves*, Silver thought as he looked around.

Alleen had already made it to the ladder on the side of the boat, and Julia gripped her arm and pulled her aboard.

Silver treaded across the water, with Shima in his grasp. When they arrived at the boat, Silver shoved his prisoner up and into the boat before climbing in himself. Alleen sat on the deck panting, and Julia stood with her Uzi pointed at Shima.

"Let's go!" she yelled toward the cockpit.

"This is my boat," Shima said.

"Shut up." Silver said to him. "Who's driving?" he asked as he glanced into the cockpit and saw Brooks at the helm. "Oh, never mind."

The yacht jerked and then droned forward. Silver pushed Shima toward the hatch before looking at Julia. "Hey, did you know these two were related?"

Julia lowered her gun. "Yeah, Alleen told me earlier."

"Of course she did." Silver turned to Alleen and nodded at Shima. "Do you still have the key for his handcuffs?"

Alleen poked in her pocket. "Yep, here," she said, producing a key.

Silver took the key. "Let's go," he said while nudging Shima to the companionway hatch.

They ducked inside and stepped down below the deck and into the cabin.

On the floor sat Miller, with his hands cuffed to a metal rod behind his back. He looked at the floor and his head bobbed as the boat bumped over the waves. The FBI agent, or ex-FBI agent at that point, didn't look over until Silver began cuffing Shima to the metal rod on the opposite side of the room.

Silver noticed him. "What? You did this to yourself."

Miller said nothing, just shook his head, and continued staring at the floor.

Silver went back to the deck, where he saw everyone under the hardtop near the cockpit. Brooks was navigating the boat while Alleen sat wrapped in a towel, with Julia's arm around her. As Silver walked toward them, he felt a shoulder ram into his arm, knocking him to the side of the boat, close to the edge. Shaking off the effects of the collision, Silver saw the muscular man approaching him with gritted teeth, knitted eyebrows, and all dripping wet. The big man threw a punch.

Silver side-stepped his opponent's punch, but the bulky man swung his other hand around and grabbed the crook between Silver's neck and shoulder. Silver pushed against the muscle man's arm but couldn't break the grip. The big man clasped Silver's throat with both hands and lifted him half a foot from the deck floor.

Silver delivered a barrage of punches to the sides of the man's head and jaws.

The burly man growled before tossing Silver through the air and sending him sliding across the deck.

As Silver struggled to his feet, he heard either Julia or

Alleen gasp and call his name. Still dazed from the fall, he turned in their direction, and before he could get his bearings, he felt the big man's arms wrap around him from behind. Silver clawed at the burly man, but his arms being forced to his sides prevented him from reaching his attacker.

Julia and Alleen scurried to the deck. Alleen stood, wide-eyed and gaping mouth, while Julia aimed her gun toward the fight.

"Lee, get out of the way!" Julia said.

"I would if I could," Silver said between grunts.

Julia moved in closer. The big guy noticed and kicked her in the gut. She fell on her back and dropped the gun.

Heat rose from Silver's stomach and into his chest. He yelled and threw his head backward, striking the big man's forehead with the back of his own. When he felt the burly guy's grip loosen, Silver kicked his leg behind himself and connected with his capturer's groin. The man released Silver and doubled over. Silver pivoted toward the muscle man and hit him with the wildest, fastest, and strongest haymaker he had thrown in a long time.

The man stood straight and stumbled backward before finding his footing and blitzing at Silver. Silver dove to the floor and grabbed the Uzi before aiming it at the man and firing three ear-rocking rounds into his chest. The big guy staggered, then fell over the back railing, hit the stern, and splashed into the water.

Silver looked in Julia's direction and saw Alleen kneeling over her and staring at him.

He shook his head. "Pirates," he said with a shrug.

Both Julia and Alleen scoffed and chuckled.

"Is everything okay back there?" Brooks asked.

"Yeah, just had to get rid of some extra weight," Silver said.

Moments later, Brooks docked the boat at the old marina. Dusk coated the sky, and the marina was crawling with cops and paramedics. Brooks sat both Shima and Miller in the back of separate squad cars while Julia and Alleen were being examined by the paramedics. They offered to check Silver, but he waved them off and told them he was fine as he stood near the back of the ambulance where Julia and Alleen sat.

"I'm so happy this is all over," Julia said.

Silver nodded.

"Is it really?" Alleen said. "He may go to jail, but will he stay there?"

"He'll get his; remember, the Yakuza is after him too," Silver said.

"How will that repair my family? Or give them relief?"

"It won't, but that's why I wanted him alive," Silver said as he noticed Brooks ending a phone call. "I'll be back," he told Julia and Alleen before walking to the FBI agent.

"Hey Silver," Brooks said. "The cops found that guy we were with earlier."

"With the tapered haircut?"

"Yep, found him half a mile up the road. They have him in custody now. Have the medics checked you out?"

"Nah, I'm okay. Can I use your phone? Mine is still drying."

"Sure, here."

Silver took the cell phone. "I'll only be a minute," he said, stepping away while dialing Anderson's number.

"Brooks?" Anderson answered.

"No, it's Silver."

"Oh, is Brooks okay?"

"Yeah, he's fine."

"How about the girls?"

"We're all fine."

"And Shima?"

"He's in custody."

"I see. Well, the FBI will bring him in, then we'll take him to one of our facilities since he's on our list and we have higher clearance."

Silver sighed. "I remember the routine," he said.

"Sure you don't want to rejoin the organization?"

"Like I told you before, I'm done with that."

"Well, it was worth a try. I'm happy everyone's okay. Good work. Now try to enjoy the rest of your vacation."

"Copy that." Silver ended the call and walked to Brooks. "Thanks," he said, handing the FBI agent the phone.

"Anytime," Brooks said.

Silver glanced at the ambulance where Julia and Alleen sat before looking in Shima's direction. "I need another favor from you," he said.

Brooks' eyebrows crinkled.

Twenty-five minutes passed, and Silver, Julia, Brooks, and Alleen were in Brooks' Ford Explorer bumping along a dirt road. Brooks sat at the wheel, Alleen sat in the front passenger seat, and Silver and Julia rode in the back seats. A pair of bright headlights tailed them the entire time. After another few minutes of driving, they arrived at a wooden gate with two armed men perched on either side. When the armed men recognized Alleen, they opened the gate and waved both Brooks and the trailing vehicle through.

"Where do I go?" Brooks asked.

"You can park near the campfire," Alleen said.

The four exited the Explorer while the other SUV parked behind them.

Polunu and Malie, along with a group of villagers, approached them.

Alleen ran to Malie and hugged her. They held each other and sobbed before pulling Polunu in and embracing him.

"Ahhh, Lee," Julia said.

Malie walked to Silver. "Thank you so much."

Silver smiled and nodded.

"How can we repay you?"

"Well, with your hospitality last night, let's just call it even."

Malie hugged Silver. "You're always welcome here," she said before hugging Julia and offering her the same sentiment. "So, what happened to Kazan?"

Silver looked at Brooks and nodded at the SUV parked behind the Ford Explorer.

Brooks waved at the vehicle and three armed men exited with a restrained Shima. The three men and Shima walked over to the group. Shima kept quiet and avoided making eye contact with anyone.

Malie shrugged. "What? You have nothing to say?"

Shima said nothing.

"Do you know how many lives you destroyed here?"

Shima remained silent.

"I was really hoping they killed you, but I think I'll feel better knowing you're rotting in jail. See, you tried to break us, but we're still here and stronger for it. You can never take that away from us."

Polunu stepped to Shima's face. "I used to look up to you," he said. "But now all I see is a pathetic excuse for a man. And you're lucky you're in the law's custody, because if you weren't, I'd kill you."

Shima stayed silent and looked at Alleen, but she turned her face from him.

"Okay, get him out of here," Brooks said, and the three men walked Shima back toward the SUV. "I'll be in the car," Brooks said to Silver and Julia before following.

Silver and Polunu shook hands.

"Thank you, you're always welcome here," Polunu said.

"Thanks, take care of yourself," Silver told him.

Polunu nodded at Silver, then Julia, before walking toward the campfire with Malie and the group of villagers.

Alleen threw her arms around Silver's chest and kissed him on the cheek. "Thank you. You helped my family heal. I'll always remember you for that," she said.

Silver smiled. "Well, I mean—my pleasure," he said.

While Julia and Alleen hugged and talked, Silver felt his phone vibrate. He stepped away and answered, "Silver."

"Is everything okay?" Semy asked.

"Yeah—yes."

"You couldn't call me back and let me know, Leroy? I've been trying to call you."

"My phone got wet again. I didn't know it started working."

"But Julia and your other friend are okay?"

"We're all fine."

Semy exhaled into the phone. "Good. I was worried, a little."

"Hey, you're amazing. There's no way I could've saved them without your help. Thank you, Semy."

"Well, what are friends for? You'd do the same for me, right?"

"Without question."

The line was silent for a couple of seconds before another voice came through.

"Is that Leroy?" Kirby's voice called.

"Oh yeah, I told Kirby about what happened. She's been worried, and angry at you."

"Great," Silver said.

"Let me talk to him," Kirby told Semy.

"Here she goes," Semy warned Silver.

"Leroy, why didn't you tell me you were in trouble?"

"It's fine."

"How can I help?"

"We're fine now."

"Why didn't you say anything?"

"I didn't want you worrying."

"As I said before, I'm not just your boss. I'm your friend. So, what do you need? I have a villa and staff there on the island."

Silver sighed. "You know, we might need a place to stay for the rest of our trip," he said.

"Awesome! I'll text you the address and let the staff know you'll be there tonight. Anything else I can do?"

"There is something I need to talk to you about."

"Sure."

"I'm not sure how much longer I'll be able to work for Cush Industries."

There was a brief silence before Kirby spoke. "Oh," she said.

"I'm not saying I want to leave now; it's just—my background makes it difficult for me to sit behind a desk or push paperwork for long. I appreciate everything you've done and love all the relationships and experiences I created during my time with the company, but I don't want you surprised when the time comes."

"Leroy, you do whatever you need to, don't worry about me or the company; we'll be fine. We're friends. I care for you beyond what you do for my company. Just know you're the best head of security I've ever had."

"I guess that settles that."

Kirby laughed, "Yeah, it does. Try to enjoy the rest of your vacation. I'll send you the address to the villa. Be safe, have fun, and I look forward to seeing you when you make it back."

"Okay boss lady, goodnight."

"Goodnight, call me when you make it to the villa."

"Sure thing, bye." Silver ended the call.

He and Julia then walked to the Explorer while Alleen stood and watched them. As they drove toward the gate, they both waved at her from the back seat, and she returned one last wave before pivoting and walking toward the campfire.

"I'm going to miss her," Julia said.

"Me too," Silver agreed.

Brooks drove them to the resort to pick up the rest of their things before dropping them off at Kirby's villa. They said goodbye to him and walked inside where a maid and chef waited for them. The staff showed them to their rooms, and they cleaned up for dinner. After the staff left for the night, Silver and Julia crashed. Silver didn't wake until late afternoon the next day. He went to Julia's room and saw her lying in bed with her eyes open.

"You awake?" he asked.

"I am," Julia said with a stretch and a yawn. "I'm ready to get back to our vacation now."

"Yeah, me too, but are you sure you're up to it?"

"Absolutely!"

Silver smiled. "What do you want to do?" he asked.

"Well... I believe there's a dinner show downtown tonight. We can go to that."

"Sounds like fun."

"But for now, I just want to get some fresh air."

The two changed their clothes and used the back door of the villa to the beach. They walked along the shore for ten minutes before stopping and looking across the water at a setting sun.

"A crazy past couple of days," Julia said.

Silver nodded. "It has definitely been an interesting vacation," he said.

The two laughed.

Julia looked down at the wet sand before staring back out at the water. "There were moments I was really scared, Lee," she said.

Silver glanced at her. "That's expected," he said.

"I thought I'd get hurt or have to hurt someone myself."

"Well, you're fine, and you wouldn't hurt a fly."

"I don't know, I almost shot Brooks."

"Really?"

"Yeah, I went down to the shore to wait for the authorities like you said, and he was there handcuffing that guy, his partner. Brooks told me who he was, but If I didn't remember you said not to shoot him, I probably would've."

"I'm happy you didn't, because I'd probably be dead too."

Julia squinted. "Oh yeah, because I don't know how to drive a boat."

They both laughed.

Julia grabbed Silver's hand and faced him. "Lee, I was really worried about you."

"I was worried about you too."

"Really?" Julia said, stepping closer, inches from his face. "I mean—how worried? On a scale of one to ten."

"I'll say a… a six and a half."

Julia stepped back and yanked her hand away from his. "A six and a half!"

Silver shrugged.

"Not even a nine, Lee?"

"A nine? I'll tell you a nine. Hanging from the back of a truck speeding down the highway. Now that's a strong nine."

Julia slapped Silver's arm. "I can't believe you," she said with a smile.

He threw his arm around her shoulders, and the two laughed and watched as the sun dipped below the horizon.

POLITICS THIEVES & BULLETS

LEROY SILVER'S ADVENTURE CONTINUES

CHAPTER ONE

THE MIDNIGHT SKY sparked glints of starry light as Leroy Silver ran to the targeted building and pressed his back against the cold wall. The five-story commercial structure sat off of a quiet city street, nestled between two taller buildings. Silver dressed in dark clothing to avoid being easily spotted, and a Glock 22 hung from his waist. Peeping around the corner, he saw a ladder, dumpster, and construction cones, but to his surprise, no guards patrolled that side of the building.

"These guys," Silver said to himself before crouch-walking along the wall.

A chalky wood smell struck his nose as he passed the dumpster and approached a door at the side of the building. He looked to his right, then his left, and his right again as he knelt at the door and turned the knob.

"Locked," he said, cocking his head. "Happy they didn't make this too easy," he continued while removing a lock pick from his pocket.

Silver spent a minute fiddling with the door before it clicked open. As he placed his hand on the knob, voices came from the opposite side of the door. He quickly pivoted and pressed his back against the wall. A second later, the door swung open, and men's voices chattered and laughed. The door hid Silver's location from the men, but he couldn't see them either. Silver stood quietly as one man walked outside, tossed something in the dumpster, then walked back inside. The men continued to laugh and talk as the door thumped closed and the lock clicked.

When the men's conversation and laughter faded, Silver turned the doorknob. "Great," he said, finding it locked.

He knelt and spent another minute unlocking it. When the door clicked open, Silver settled his lock pick inside his pocket and opened the door a slit. An air-conditioned breeze swept across his face when he peeked inside. He entered a semi-bright, spotless commercial kitchen. Stoves, freezers, and the appliances looked new. The ceramic-tiled floor was pristine, and the vibrant coat of paint smelled freshly applied.

Silver scanned the kitchen and noticed an office on the opposite end. He crouched-walked to it and ducked inside. The darkened room consisted of a desk, a few chairs, and a filing cabinet. Noticing a breaker box on the far wall, Silver crept across the vinyl flooring to it. Just as he stood to reach for the box, footsteps knocked on the kitchen floor. Silver crouched and hid behind the filing cabinet as a man in a dark-blue guard uniform and boots entered the office and glanced the space over. Silver inched further into the corner behind the cabinet. After a moment, he peeked around the cabinet and saw the guard standing in the kitchen with his back to the office's doorway. Removing his Glock 22, Silver aimed the gun at the man and lightly tapped the trigger twice.

"Hey, what are you doing?" a voice asked.

The guard looked to his left. "Comin'," he said before disappearing in that direction.

Silver holstered his gun, then stood and opened the breaker box. He saw many breakers, but he was interested in the three labeled *lobby camera*, *server room 2nd fl*, and *2nd fl cameras*. He flicked the breakers off for the cameras and exited the office, making the same left the guard did just moments before. Passing through flapping doors, he entered an area and found a large counter with a kiosk on top. Silver circled the counter and threaded between a few dining tables on his way into the lobby. He noticed the disabled camera above and remained in the shadows and close to the wall while crossing the lobby. Walking past the elevators, he entered the stairwell and hiked to the second floor.

As Silver approached the door, he heard talking from above. He pressed against the wall, then peeked around the steps and saw another guard, dressed the same as the last, but slightly taller. The man held a cellphone to his ear and shrugged before raising his free hand.

"What do you want from me? I have to work," he said into the phone. "Yeah, I know, but someone has to cover the shift."

As the man continued to talk on the phone, Silver removed his pistol and aimed it at the man's back. He tapped the trigger twice, then settled his back against the wall and waited.

"Bye," the guard said a moment later. He put his phone away then said, "She's gonna be the death of me."

After hearing the door above open then shut, Silver opened the door for the second floor. He entered an empty, dimly lit hall with carpeted floors. At the end of the hall were double wooden doors.

"I bet that's where it's at," Silver said to himself.

In a crouch, he crept down the hall, passing closed doors on either side as he did. A humming sound hit his ears when he made it halfway, and the noise increased with every step he took toward the double doors. He jiggled the knobs, but the doors were locked. Scanning them, Silver didn't find any panels or electronic locking mechanisms, so he removed his pick and opened the lock. Inside the room, the humming intensified, and the temperature dropped. Silver shut the door behind himself and peered down an aisle of server racks. As he continued across the polished concrete floor, the servers and computer network equipment buzzed at him from either side. Silver inspected each rack until he found what he was looking for. A computer terminal for the main storage server.

Silver removed a thumb drive from his pocket and inserted it into the computer. As he hovered his fingers over the keyboard to type, air whooshed over the hissing computer equipment. He ducked and crept toward the front of the room. Peeping between racks, he saw a guard entering with his hand rested on his holstered pistol. As the man walked down the aisle, Silver removed his gun and aimed it at him. Silver tapped the trigger twice, then returned to the terminal and typed on the keyboard. He dragged the mouse around and clicked a few buttons. The terminal's monitor displayed a green status bar and a file transferring to his thumb drive.

"Who are you?" Silver heard from his left. "Freeze—put your hands in the air."

Silver looked at the guard. "Which one is it? Freeze or put my hands in the air?"

The guard cocked his head to the side, and his eyebrows furrowed. "Mr.—Mr. Silver."

"Yep," Silver said, turning to the terminal's monitor.

"Sir, what are you doing here?" the guard asked while holstering his firearm.

"I'm stealing some confidential files."

"Huh? Wait—is the physical security test today?"

Silver nodded at the screen.

"I didn't know that'd be tonight."

Silver glanced at the man. "Wouldn't be much of a test if you knew I was coming," he told him.

The guard sighed and dropped his head before looking up. "Well, at least I caught you," he said.

Silver shook his head. "Nope. You're dead," he said.

"What? When?"

"Just now when you walked into the room."

"Oh," the guard said with his gaze bouncing off the floor, then to Silver's face. "So, if Jones and Fisher don't catch you, we fail."

The folder finished copying, and Silver removed his thumb drive from the computer before turning to the guard. "Jones and Fisher are dead too. Jones in the stairwell, and Fisher in the kitchen."

The guard lowered his head. "Oh boy," he said with a sigh.

Silver stepped to him. "It's okay. I understand this facility isn't fully operational, and the security infrastructure isn't in place yet."

The guard lifted his head and nodded.

"But I want you guys alert at all times," Silver said. "I should've never made it up here, especially since this is my first time in the building. I'll be sending over some additional training documents and providing some classes for you guys."

"Yes, sir," the guard said before tilting his head toward the walkie-talkie strapped to his shoulder.

Silver pivoted and walked toward the door, and as he did, he heard the guard's radio scratch, then beep.

"Fisher, Jones. Our head of security is here. He's on his way down, so keep a lookout for him."

Silver exited the server room and entered the stairwell. Before he took the first step down, he heard footsteps from above thumping toward him.

"Jones," he said as the man approached.

"Mr. Silver, sir," Jones replied.

"When you're entering the stairwell, you want to do so quietly."

Jones nodded.

"And make sure you check all the stairwell levels. There aren't that many floors," Silver said before continuing toward the first floor.

"Yes, sir," Jones said.

Silver entered the first floor and scanned near the elevators and around the lobby on his way toward the front door. When he made it halfway across the lobby, Fisher walked to him.

"Is everything okay, sir?" the guard asked.

"Yeah," Silver said. "Just looking to see where some additional cameras can be installed. You're on the first floor tonight, right?"

"Yes, sir."

"Okay. There's a breaker box in the kitchen's office. I'm gonna recommend we move it to a locked closet, but for now, make sure you pay close attention to that area."

"Copy that, sir."

"I know we don't have a gate yet or all the cameras installed outside, but make sure you check the parameter," Silver said before pointing toward the kitchen. "And remember, that side door opens outward. Keep that in mind while you're patrolling the parameter."

"Got it," Fisher said.

Silver stared at him for a moment before sighing, then turning toward the front door.

"Do you need me to call you a car, sir?" Fisher said.

"No, I'll take care of it," Silver said, turning the door's locking mechanism and prying the doors apart with his hands. He stepped through, then pulled the doors together. "Lock the door," he said to Fisher.

The guard nodded before walking to the door and turning the lock. Silver heard a click and raised his thumb to the man before walking across the street and two blocks to a busy intersection where he hailed a cab.

Twelve minutes later, Silver was cruising through Downtown Manhattan. Headlights and car horns blared as the cab driver veered off the street and parked at a curb.

"Thanks," Silver said before handing the driver a few bills, exiting the car, then stepping onto a sidewalk.

As the cab darted into traffic, Silver walked along the sidewalk, threading around some pedestrians on his way to his destination. McLarens. A cozy sports bar he found years ago while on an assignment when he worked for the government. He stood at the corner, about ten yards away from the sports bar, and watched the front door. It was two a.m. and patrons were leaving the establishment. Some casually while others stumbled out laughing and having loud conversations.

Silver watched the door for another ten minutes before seeing who he was waiting for. A fit, light-skinned woman with long, dark, curly hair exited the bar with another woman and man.

"Jules," Silver said to himself as the woman spoke to her colleagues.

After a minute, she waved goodbye to them, then stuck her hand out for a cab. Silver took a step forward in her direction, but stopped when he felt a tight sensation in his gut. *Maybe now isn't the best time,* he thought before stepping back and watching as the woman entered a cab and then drove off.

The next morning, Silver woke to the sun warming his face. He leaned forward and looked at his clock. The display showed 10:17 a.m.

"Great, I'm late," he said, springing from the bed and darting to the bathroom.

It took him twenty minutes to wash up and to throw on a pair of jeans, a t-shirt, and a jacket, then another twenty minutes to make it to his office building. As he walked toward the front entrance, the doors slid apart, and he stepped into a spacious lobby. Silver dodged a few walking suits and skirts on his way toward the elevator. He made it halfway before he heard his name called from the security station at the center of the lobby.

"Mr. Silver," the voice said.

Silver turned to find a fair-skinned, pudgy man in a security uniform approaching him.

"What's up, Greg?" Silver said, before pivoting and continuing toward the elevators.

"Hi, boss," Greg said, while walking next to him. "I heard

from the guys at the new location. They said you stopped by early this morning—"

"Yeah."

"They feel it wasn't a fair test, considering the building's security infrastructure is only around seventy-five percent complete."

Silver chuckled. "What are you, their spokesman?" he said while pressing the up arrow button on the elevator's panel. The button turned red, and the elevator's car thumped and hummed from above.

Greg shrugged, then smiled.

"Doesn't matter if the security infrastructure isn't complete," Silver said. "They should know if someone is inside the building."

"Well, they're worried about their jobs."

Silver shook his head as the elevator dinged and the doors opened. "I see it as a failure on my part," he said, entering the empty elevator and pressing the button for the sixth floor. "But if you don't get back to your station, you may get fired," Silver said jokingly.

Greg smiled and turned toward the lobby as the elevator doors closed. The elevator droned non-stop to the sixth floor before jerking to a stop and whizzing open. Silver exited onto a marble floor and walked toward the receptionist's desk.

"Hi, Leroy," greeted a smiling brunette with long hair and dimples.

Silver returned the smile. "Good morning, Stacey," he said, while performing a salute. "Is Kirby in?"

"Yes, she's in her office. I'll let her know you're coming."

"Thanks," Silver said, before walking past Stacey's desk and down a hall.

Offices and conference rooms flanked him on either side as he walked to glass-frosted French doors at the end of the hall. The sign next to the door read *Kirby Cush, CEO*. Silver knocked twice before opening the door and poking his head inside. The marble floor continued into the office, and near the back, an executive desk sat on an area rug. A woman with long blonde hair sat at the desk with the phone to her ear.

"You are so funny," she said into the phone before noticing Silver and waving him in with a smile.

Silver stepped inside and strolled past a couch, bookshelf, and a huddle room before dodging a chair in front of the desk and taking a seat.

"Guess who just walked into my office?" she said into the phone. "Why don't you ask him?" she continued before pressing a button on the phone's station and placing the handset on the hook.

"Hi, Leroy," a soft, but assertive voice came through the phone's speaker.

Silver sighed while leaning toward the phone. "Hi Semy," he said.

"Kirby and I were just talking about you."

Silver glanced at Kirby.

She shrugged while placing her hand over her mouth to conceal her laughter.

Silver looked at the phone. "What else is new?" he said. "So, what exactly were you two talking about?"

"Just your love life."

Silver shared his gaze between Kirby and the phone. "Really?" he said with a chuckle. "Because you two are experts in that area, right?"

"I have men hit on me all the time," Kirby said. "As a matter of fact, I have a date with a gentleman tonight."

"And I'm meeting someone this weekend," said Semy's voice through the speaker.

"Well," Silver said, leaning back in his chair. "Both of you do a good job of hiding these men, because I haven't heard about or seen a one of 'em."

"We don't tell you all our business, Leroy."

Silver scoffed. "And yet you're always in mine," he said.

Kirby cocked her head to the side and looked at Silver.

He shrugged.

"We're just trying to help," Semy said.

"Yeah," Kirby said. "We've noticed a difference in you since you two haven't been talking."

"What are you talking about?" Silver quickly said.

Kirby patted the air between them. "Calm down. We talked to her and—"

Silver stood from his chair. "You got to be kidding me," he said with a slight chuckle. "You guys actually talked to her."

"Yeah," Semy said. "We've been hanging out with her."

Kirby shrugged. "She's our friend too," she told Silver.

Silver pointed at Kirby, then at the phone. "Look. I knew the two of you ran together, but I didn't know you initiated Jules into your pack."

"You should talk to her."

"Yeah," Semy followed up. "You two like each other and spent a lot of time together, but never even kissed."

Silver slapped his forehead and chuckled as he plopped into his chair.

"A girl can only wait so long for you to take action," Semy continued.

"Alright, okay," Silver said while fanning his hands in the air. "Semy, isn't the NYPD paying you to catch bad guys —not to harass me?"

"Shut up, Leroy. It's called concern, and I'm on a break. Plus, they may not be paying me much of anything if they cut our funding."

"Oh, how's Bennett doing? I haven't talked to him in a while."

"Your old military buddy," Kirby chimed in. "I haven't spoken to him since he recommended you work for me," she said to Silver.

"Um," Semy sighed through the speaker. "That's a really good question because I haven't seen him a lot lately. I believe he's busy with a joint FBI case."

"Hmm. Well, next time you run into him, tell 'em he owes me a call."

"I'll think about it, Leroy. Look, I gotta get back to it, so I'll talk with you guys later—and Kirby."

"Yeah," Kirby said while arching toward the phone.

"Let me know how the date goes."

"Of course."

"Alright, talk with you later, girl. Bye, Leroy."

"Bye, little-big-mouth," Silver said to Semy before Kirby pressed a button on the phone, ending the call.

She looked at Silver. "You're mean," she said, smiling.

Silver's eyebrows rose. "I'm mean?" he asked while pointing at himself. "You guys are in my business, talking behind my back."

"Ah stop it. We just care."

"Anyway."

"You had something you wanted to talk to me about?"

Silver adjusted in his chair. "Yeah," he said. "There are several security vulnerabilities we'll have to address at the new location."

Kirby furrowed her eyebrows. "Parts of that building are

still under construction. I don't think we've even installed an alarm system yet," she said.

"Right, but there are some things we can address before then."

"Like?"

"More cameras on the parameter and in the lobby. Moving the breaker box from the first floor. And some training for the security guards."

Kirby shrugged. "Okay, you're the expert," she said. "And you haven't steered me wrong yet. I say it all the time. I trust you."

"I'll put together a document detailing my findings," Silver said while standing.

"Wait. Did you go to the new location yesterday after you'd already worked for twelve hours?"

Silver hunched his shoulders. "Yeah. I guess so."

Kirby shook her head and sighed. "Take the rest of the day off."

Silver cocked his head and pursed his lips.

"Don't give me that look," she said. "I don't need my head of security overworked. I need him fresh."

"I assure you, I'm—"

Kirby raised her palm to Silver. "I don't want to hear it. It's an order, sir. I'll relay your findings to the multiple security managers we have, and they can follow up on your concerns."

Silver inhaled, then opened his mouth but said nothing. He wasn't sure what to say. He didn't feel tired and recalled working an assignment for his old unit with the government that required him to stay awake for thirty hours straight. But he no longer worked for the government and didn't care to, so figured it wouldn't hurt to take some time off. He'd just have to find something to do to occupy himself.

"Yes, ma'am," he finally said to Kirby.

"Okay. I'll see you later tomorrow at the earliest," she said.

"Copy that," Silver said, before walking to the door. "Oh yeah," he said with his hand on the doorknob, and facing Kirby. "Enjoy your date."

Kirby squinted. "What does that mean?" she asked while smiling.

Silver smirked. "It means enjoy your date," he said.

Kirby laughed. "Bye. Get out of here."

Silver left the office, took the elevator to the lobby, and exited the building. As he walked to an intersection near the end of the block, his phone vibrated in his pocket. He removed it and saw that he had three missed calls within the last twenty minutes, all from Jon Bennett.

Silver pressed his phone's screen and held it to his ear. After a few rings, a somewhat fast baritone voice jumped on the line.

"Silver, Silver," Bennett said.

"Hey man, we were just talking about y—" Silver started.

"Silver, I need a favor," Bennett interrupted. "Can we meet?"

THANK YOU FOR READING

I have a favor to ask. If you have a moment, I would really appreciate it if you could leave a short review on the page where you purchased this book. I'm thankful for you sharing your feedback about this book. It really helps new readers find this series.

Sign up for notifications of new books by Alex Cage and exclusive giveaways

www.AlexCage.com/signup

ALSO BY ALEX CAGE

More books by Alex Cage. Have you read them all? Grab your next adventure today!

Leroy Silver Series

Contracts & Bullets

Aloha & Bullets

Politics Thieves & Bullets

Orlando Black Series

Carolina Dance

Bayside Boom

Bet on Black

Get the latest releases and exclusive giveaways, sign up to the Alex Cage Reader List.

www.AlexCage.com/signup

JOIN THE READER'S LIST

Get the latest releases and exclusive giveaways - sign up to the Alex Cage Reader List:

www.AlexCage.com/signup

ABOUT THE AUTHOR

Alex Cage is a thriller author and passionate wordsmith who loves to blend his fascination with martial arts and travel with high-octane action and explosive adventures. He enjoys nothing more than entertaining his readers with death-defying missions, larger-than-life characters, and suspenseful stories that always find a way to keep you on your toes.

As the author of nearly a dozen titles, including the Orlando Black series and the Leroy Silver series, Alex combines his obsession for thrillers with a sprinkling of fantasy and sci-fi, so that readers will always find something to capture their imagination. He currently resides in North Carolina. When not writing his next novel, you can find him reading and practicing martial arts.

Find out more about Alex Cage (and get a free read):

www.alexcage.com
connect@alexcage.com

ALEX CAGE
CLEAN FAST-PACED ACTION THRILLERS